# A Strange and Sublime Address

# Amit Chaudhuri

faber

First published in the UK by William Heinemann Ltd in 1991

This paperback edition first published in 2022
by Faber & Faber Ltd
Bloomsbury House
74–77 Great Russell Street
London WC1B 3DA

Typeset by Faber & Faber Ltd
Printed in the UK by CPI Group (UK) Ltd, Croydon, CR0 4YY

A CIP record for this book
is available from the British Library

ISBN 978–0–571–36149–6

MIX
Paper from
responsible sources
FSC® C013604

2 4 6 8 10 9 7 5 3 1

*To my parents*

# Foreword

'Sandeep, meanwhile, had come to the conclusion that the grown-ups were mad, each after his or her own fashion. Simple situations were turned into complex dramatic ones; not until then did everybody feel important and happy.' In Amit Chaudhuri's *A Strange and Sublime Address*, Sandeep is a small boy, an only child who lives in a Bombay high-rise and who, with his parents, makes two long visits to his extended family in Calcutta. The book is the story of the atmosphere in the small house in Calcutta that they visit. Twenty-five years after its initial publication, Chaudhuri's novel about a young boy's view of family life and the world around him seems as elegant and exquisite and original as it did on its initial publication.

Sandeep watches his relatives, his parents, the servants and the neighbours, alert to everything – sounds,

smells, domestic habits, moods, weather, plants. He is vastly amused by tiny details such as his uncle's car, which breaks down, his bustling morning rituals. He spends most of the time, however, with his two cousins and with the women in the family. He notices the women's clothes and perfumes with relish; he listens to their voices in a way that suggests both a curious child and a budding novelist. He registers what happens precisely and carefully; the rhythms of the book follow the faded happiness of things and the strange, remembered moments, but render them as urgent, present, almost pure.

Sandeep is smart, and Chaudhuri is clever enough and talented enough to let his observations stand for a lot, to let what he sees and hears become the drama of the book. He also manages a tonal high-wire act by convincing the reader that this is the world that a child observed, a child who knows no more than a child might – but also that it is remembered using the prism of a child's gaze by a writer in possession of a rich prose style, a writer who does not wish to comment much, or offer analysis or additions.

The book, then, is both knowing and unknowing; the events are both experienced with immediacy and remembered with grace and care, but without

nostalgia or too much easy humour. Chaudhuri wishes
to evoke the past, and that is done not only with an
undertone of sadness at the notion that these things
are over, but with a relish arising from the power of
what is remembered, the force of its detail, its physical-
ity, its immediacy. Something that happened in child-
hood in this book takes on all the glittering excitement
and precision of the present, as though memory itself
can be more truthful and pressing than experience, or
as though memory itself were, indeed, a kind of rich
experience.

There are moments of evocative beauty in the novel,
such as the family's visit to the elderly relatives, the
presence of a new baby, a rainstorm, the uncle's illness,
his time in hospital and his recovery. The book depends
on its own tones and textures rather than on twists of
fate or plot. It allows the act of evocation itself to have a
sort of narrative energy.

The strange and sublime address is given as the
house in Calcutta, followed by the names of the outer
world, ending with Asia, and then Earth, and then
the Solar System, and then the Universe. This echoes
Chapter 1 of *A Portrait of the Artist as a Young Man*
by James Joyce, in which Stephen Dedalus gives his
address in almost similar terms. Joyce's book deals

with the growth of Stephen, who is viewed with the same earnestness with which Stephen might have viewed himself, as well as a glaze of irony – that of an author watching over his subject years later, as he sets out on his road to freedom.

Stephen Dedalus's world in Joyce's novel is both his private consciousness and the public life of his country. The tension between Ireland and England or between Catholic doctrine and liberalism are as fully part of the narrative as Stephen's private perceptions or his arguments with himself. These tensions matter to Stephen emotionally; they become part of the nets that have him captured and which he must fly from. *A Portrait of the Artist* moves deftly between the public and the private, between 'the smithy of the soul' and the 'conscience of the race'. Joyce allows Stephen's experience to embody Ireland as much as reject it or evade it.

In Chaudhuri's book, on the other hand, although politics and a sense of public affairs are allowed into the narrative, they are there glancingly, as part of the flavour of things, and are no more important than anything else. For a foreign reader, *A Strange and Sublime Address* is fascinating because it does not dramatise the legacy of Partition, or deal with the caste system in India, or use the novel to enrich our knowledge of

large questions of identity and politics. The book normalises and domesticates what is often presented as exotic or even alarming.

Chaudhuri allows his characters a presence that is fully personal, that is freely their own, rather than offering them to us as examples of what India is like now, or what colonialism has done. He does full justice to them within the limits of the actual world they inhabit. Because his impulse is essentially poetic or cinematic rather than political, these limits cease to matter – they blur at the edges or become insignificant under the pressure of acute observation and carefully controlled cadence.

Something of a similar nature happens in John McGahern's book, *Memoir*, as the world of the child in relation to what is around him is captured in elaborate detail and with the effortless grace of a serious prose stylist. But the brightness which memory evokes in McGahern's book serves only to make the darkness of the book sharper and more poignant. *Memoir* is not only about the pain of time passing, but the pain of what actually happened at the time. Such bitter shadows also appear in Joyce's novel. In both of these books, some of the energy comes from the way in which the idyll of childhood and the innocence of

youth are disturbed by adult indifference or by cruelty.

What distinguishes Chaudhuri's book is his concern with happiness, the hardest subject of all for the writer of fiction. It would have been simple in his book to bring in the drama of family conflict or some nightmare images of poverty and destitution. Instead, *A Strange and Sublime Address* is concerned to register ease and fullness, but without nostalgia or sentimentality or false pleading. The evocations of ease and tolerance are captured in the tone of the prose itself, the unstretched and languid style, the exact and unforced descriptions, the mildly amused ironic undertones.

In other evocative and poetic books which deal with images of childhood – books such as *The Diary of Helena Morley*, translated from the Portuguese by Elizabeth Bishop, or some sections of Jean-Paul Sartre's *The Words*, or Emmanuelle Guattari's *I, Little Asylum*, or the moments in Proust which deal with the boy and his grandmother at Balbec – there is also a sense of tender particularity, of the need to write down what it was like so that those rooms and voices will not fade, will not be forgotten. The power rests in that urge to remember, capture and hold. The greater the precision, it seems, the more the book propels that power outwards, to the reader who knew nothing

of the particular moment but feels and shares the impulse to record.

What is universal in this context is the battle between innocence and experience. Each thing seen and noticed, no matter how innocently, adds to the richness of the self. When Chaudhuri sees saris being washed by a servant, for example, he writes: 'Later, she would wring the saris into long, exhausted pythons of cloth.' This very act of noticing moves the boy from mere observer to consummate describer; making metaphors allows both him and the reader to see more clearly. The boy's mind appears more complex as it takes the world in. He becomes an emerging character in his own fiction.

As the experience of seeing and registering continues, a sort of innocence is maintained in Chaudhuri's book. When the boys see the pigeons mating, for example, they can make no sense of the movements, although the reader can. And then there is the matter of time, which is the essential theme of a book in which the writer imagines a Bengal returning 'to that original darkness', untouched by time, a 'Bengal of the bullock-cart and the earthen lamp'. And the urge to slow down moments, such as at meals when there is a sudden silence, 'a gap of hushed clarity', as though the camera of the novel stopped, or the clock stopped,

or memory froze a single moment that is gone.

What happens to time in the book is not merely that it fades, it is also remembered. Memory, then, as much as time, slowly becomes Chaudhuri's governing theme. One of the characters is brought back in time by taste: 'Each time he put a small dollop of the yoghurt in his mouth, and chewed on the khoi patiently he tasted his childhood. It was made of the sourness of yoghurt, the sweetness of sugar, and the grey taste of bananas. Also the warmth of his mother's fingers from which he ate the mixture. It was as if his memory resided in the small, invisible taste buds in his tongue rather than in his brain.'

But what is at the heart of the enterprise is delicacy. Chaudhuri handles how things looked and felt and sounded not only with the attention of a born noticer, but also with supreme tact. The drama comes in the phrasing, as though the book had found a melody early on which not only evoked this world of children and family and servants and the city, but represented the essence of things and then transformed them into beauty, much as a painter might, or a singer, but in ways that are oddly rare in prose narrative and all the more sublime for that.

Colm Tóibín, Dublin, 2016

Note: the word 'mama', in Bengali, and presumably any other North Indian language, means 'maternal uncle'. Different prefixes may be attached to this word, to describe and categorize the different types of maternal uncles that exist in this world. For instance, 'chhoto' means 'small' or 'young'; therefore, 'Chhotomama' in the story means 'Junior Uncle'. Chhotomama's wife is called 'Mamima' in the story; this may be roughly translated as 'motherly maternal aunt'. Children are usually addressed by their nicknames; these may or may not have a meaning. All in all, the Bengali family is a tangled web, an echoing cave, of names and appellations, too complicated to explain individually. Their meaning, hopefully, is brought out in context.

# 1

He saw the lane. Small houses, unlovely and unremarkable, stood face to face with each other. Chhotomama's house had a pomelo tree in its tiny courtyard and madhavi creepers by its windows. A boy stood clinging to the rusting iron gate, while another boy pushed it backward and forward. As he did so, the first boy travelled in a small arc through space. When the taxi stopped in front of the house, they stared at it with great dignity for a few moments, then ran off in terror, leaving the gate swinging mildly and illegally. A window opened above (it was so silent for a second that Sandeep could hear someone unlocking it) and Babla's face appeared behind the mullions.

Chhotomama and Saraswati, the maidservant, came down and helped them with their bags. Sandeep ran up the stairs with his cousins, not looking back. There was a

thrilled impatience about his movements, as if he either wanted to finish or begin something quickly. His aunt, by contrast, stood at the head of the stairs, in a place that was half sunlit and half shadowy, with immaculate serenity, seemingly not having moved from where she had said goodbye to him about a year ago; she said:

'How have you been, Mona?'

When she saw Sandeep's mother, she went down the stairs and grasped her hand in a relaxed way; all the excitement shone in her eyes.

'Didi . . .' she said.

They went up in a procession, Abhi, Babla, Sandeep, his mother, his uncle, his aunt, as if they were going up to a shrine on pilgrimage. Later, they sat on a wide bed beneath an ancient fan which, as it rotated, moved unreliably from side to side, like a great bird trying to fly. The holiday-mood transported them with its poetry; they could have been anywhere—on a hillside on the Western Ghats or in a cave in Kanheri. Sandeep's mother now opened a suitcase and distributed gifts she had brought from Bombay.

Gleaming objects, clothes, perfumes, emerged from the suitcase.

'And here are saris for you,' she said to Sandeep's aunt. 'Though Calcutta saris are the loveliest.'

'Oh but these are beautiful,' replied Mamima, unravelling a sari, which broke out into a galaxy of hand-woven stars, a cosmos of streaking comets and symbolic blue horizons.

'She's right,' said Chhotomama. 'Calcutta saris *are* the loveliest. Though this is nice,' he said grudgingly, touching the cloth.

Near them, Sandeep and Abhi silently wrestled with each other, looking vaguely like the two angry, rumpled pillows at the head of the bed. The grown-ups, who made a little shifting arena around their bodies, paid them scarcely more attention than they paid the pillows. Both arms pinned down, Abhi stared into Sandeep's eyes in mock exhaustion and with a distant affection.

'Give up?' cried Sandeep.

'No,' whispered Abhi. 'No I don't give up.'

Irreconcilable as two conflicting principles, they fell to struggling again. It was, actually, an excuse for embracing, touching, exploring each other's presence; not having met for a year, they, great friends, wanted to do these things, and fighting seemed the only acceptable way towards intimacy. Babla, meanwhile, sat listening to the adults talking; his eyes darted from one face to the other, then back again, as if he were following a game of tennis, as if he could see questions and answers,

3

like white balls being tossed from one end of the court to another.

The morning passed in a wave of words. Sandeep's mother talked about Bombay, about Sandeep's father's responsibilities in 'the company', about how he worked too hard, and how he never had time to go anywhere. Chhotomama, whose problems were more ordinary and also more difficult to solve, loved listening to the remote complaints of his sister's life, objecting to or agreeing with, now and then, a phrase. Sandeep, an only child, felt the shared background of brother and brother, and brother and sister, throw upon him a shade as that of the cool, expansive branches of a rooted banyan tree. He wandered in the shade, forgetting it was temporary. Mamima brought his mother and Chhotomama cups of tea, which they stirred thoughtfully in the middle of a discussion; Saraswati went to the market and returned with a large, dark boal fish for lunch. The grown-ups never fell short of subjects for discussion; in the kitchen, as Saraswati worked, the pots and pans also held a different, but no less urgent, dialogue. Sandeep, doing something or the other with his cousins, gradually adjusted his senses to Chhotomama's house, to the pale walls, the spider-webs in the corners, the tranquil bedsheets on the old beds, the portraits of grandfathers

and grandmothers, the fans that swung drunkenly from side to side—all so different from the quiet and perfected apartment he lived in in Bombay.

After they had exhausted all their games, they had a bath. They stood naked in front of the bathroom; their clothes lay in a heap at their feet; their testicles hung silently and insignificantly like small, unplucked fruit. Babla's penis was hardly visible, a sleeping beetle everyone had forgotten to notice. He wasn't aware that anything unusual had happened; having spent only six years on this planet, clothes were still a relatively puzzling and uncomfortable phenomenon to him.

Mamima now kneaded Abhi's and Babla's bodies with mustard-oil. She twisted them, took them apart, put them together; they surrendered to her as plasticine surrenders its infinite forms to a child's fingers. When she rubbed an arm or leg, it appeared to detach itself from the body, with a wonderful absence of pain, and come into her skilful hands, a live, grotesque appendage. She would oil it till it shone, and then fix it, with a grim, satisfied smile, where it belonged.

A sharp aura of mustard-oil flowered, giving Sandeep's nostrils a faraway sentient pleasure—it wasn't a sweet smell, but there was a harsh unexpectedness about

it he liked. It reminded him of sunlight. In Bengal, both tamarind and babies are soaked in mustard-oil, and then left upon a mat on the terrace to absorb the morning sun. The tamarind is left out till it dries up and shrivels into an inimitable flavour and a ripe old age; but the babies are brought in before it gets too hot, and then bathed in cool water. With their frantic miniature limbs and their brown, shining bodies, they look like little koi fish caught from the Hooghly river, struggling into life.

The bathroom was a small square room, with a basin on one side, and a window on the right. The window-sill was cluttered with shampoos and soaps and unguents. On the other side of the closed window, pigeons sat through their afternoons with a serene lack of urgency, and sometimes shifted to look in uncuriously at a nude bather. One could hear mynahs and shaliks singing outside, though one could hear their fragmentary chorus more clearly from the toilet, which was next to the bath. An obsessive, busy music repeated itself behind the frosted glass. Sometimes, one heard the shrill cries of their young, and felt surrounded and safe.

There was a tap in the middle; at the top, a round eye sprinkled with orifices protruded from a pipe that was bent downward like the neck of a tired giraffe; this was the shower. There was no hot water and no bathtub, but

no one seemed to miss what was not there. Sometimes, in the afternoon, Saraswati would wash saris and sheets, tedious yards of cloth, beneath the running tap, sitting fixedly on her haunches, rubbing the clothes, banging them repeatedly with a loud watery 'pluff' on the floor. As she banged them, the bathroom echoed with a strange rhythm. Later, she would wring the saris into long, exhausted pythons of cloth. She would notice the boys observing her with dark, inquisitive eyes from behind the door, and she would say:

'What are you looking at, you hooligans?'

When they had had their bath, they trooped out like naked ruffians on an island, spattering the floor with their wet footprints. Later they went down to have lunch in the dining room; they dangled their feet ferociously from chairs round a large, shabby table with pots thronging in the centre.

Pieces of boal fish, cooked in turmeric, red chilli paste, onions and garlic, lay in a red, fiery sauce in a flat pan; rice, packed into an even white cake, had a spade-like spoon embedded in it; slices of fried aubergine were arranged on a white dish; dal was served from another pan with a drooping ladle; long, complex filaments of banana-flower, exotic, botanical, lay in yet another pan

in a dark sauce; each plate had a heap of salt on one side, a green chilli, and a slice of sweet-smelling lemon. The grown-ups snapped the chillies (each made a sound terse as a satirical retort), and scattered the tiny, deadly seeds in their food. If any of the boys were ever brave or foolish enough to bite a chilli, their eyes filled tragically with tears, and they longed to drown in a cool, clear lake. Though Chhotomama was far from affluent, they ate well, especially on Sundays, caressing the rice and the sauces on their plates with attentive, sensuous fingers, fingers which performed a practised and graceful ballet on the plate till it was quite empty.

# 2

Later, after washing their hands, they went up to the second and topmost storey of the house. Sandeep's mother and Mamima reclined on the large bed. Their conversation was a transparent stream that occasionally trickled into desert patches of silence. Chhotomama turned on the radio, which began to babble immediately like the local idiot:

'Both grandson and grandfather love eating Thin Arrowroot Biscuits.'

'Nothing's as kind to your skin as Boroline Antiseptic Cream.'

He lay back on the small bed, secure as a soldier in his trench, with the newspaper in his hands; he folded it several ways and made it crackle festively. His face and his arms drowned in the black and white ocean of the

newspaper, surfacing intermittently. Sighing regretfully, Chhotomama fell asleep, the newspaper covering his face. When the breath came up from his nostrils, the newspaper rose and fell lightly, as if it were breathing as well. On the big bed, Mamima and Sandeep's mother began to dream, sprawled in vivid crab-like postures. His aunt lay on her stomach, her arms bent as if she were swimming to the edge of a lake; his mother lay on her back, her feet (one of which had a scar on it) arranged in the joyous pose of a dancer.

A mournful song now came on the radio. It was an old radio, a wedding-gift, shaped like a box, with outdated knobs and dials. When Sandeep was younger, he had thought there were little men, talented homunculi, inside the box of the radio, who performed those songs. But that seemed long ago. Beside the radio, there was a clock with a white face which always ran ten minutes fast. Every night, the time was readjusted, and every morning, with great accuracy, it had gained ten minutes. At about half past four, when the clock said twenty to five, the grown-ups woke and stretched their arms like reluctant children. The Sunday lunch, then the Sunday nap—and the thought of Monday, that difficult day, was aborted. The radio crackled with the nervous, breathless sound of football commentary;

dust had settled on the floor and furniture of the house.

Calcutta is a city of dust. If one walks down the street, one sees mounds of dust like sand-dunes on the pavements, on which children and dogs sit doing nothing, while sweating labourers dig into the macadam with spades and drills. The roads are always being dug up, partly to construct the new underground railway system, or perhaps for some other obscure reason, such as replacing a pipe that doesn't work with another pipe that doesn't work. At such times, Calcutta is like a work of modern art that neither makes sense nor has utility, but exists for some esoteric aesthetic reason. Trenches and mounds of dust everywhere give the city a strange bombed-out look. The old houses, with their reposeful walls, are crumbling to slow dust, their once-gleaming gates are rusting. Dust flakes off the ceilings in offices; the buildings are becoming dust, the roads are becoming dust. At the same time, dust is constantly raised into startling new shapes and unexpected forms by the arbitrary workings of the wind, forms on which dogs and children sit doing nothing. Daily, Calcutta disintegrates, unwhispering, into dust, and daily it rises from dust again.

A house in Calcutta must be swept and scrubbed at least twice a day. Once, in the morning, Saraswati polished

the floor with a moist rag, and Mamima religiously dusted the tables and chairs. The dust rose in the air in breathless clouds and seemed to evaporate and disappear. But by evening, it would condense, like moisture, and resettle on the surfaces of things. A little before sunset, a woman called Chhaya came to clean the house a second time, smiling at the boys as they waited impatiently for her to finish. She had a serious cultured face with a serious smile, the face of a kindly and understanding teacher; it was hard to believe she lived across the railway-lines, in the clump of huts called the basti, from which whiffs of excrement rose on windy days.

She would sweep the floor—unending expanses, acres and acres of floor—with a short broom called the jhadu, swiping away the dust in an arc with its long tail, which reminded one of the drooping tail of some nameless, exotic bird. She would collect the dust in a corner, and here there would be an accumulation of unlikely treasure that had blown in from outside or had gathered, unnoticed, inside: a single elegant pigeon's feather, a page lost from a book, a dead spider which ants had forgotten to carry off, the long, black, tender loops of Mamima's and Sandeep's mother's hair.

Then she would dip a grey rag into a pail, and sit on her haunches at one end of the room, and swish

the rag around the floor. Carefully, deliberately, she would begin to advance to the other end of the room, swiping the floor with the moist rag, her right arm moving regularly and automatically, like a fin, till she had reached the other end. Her odd movement forward on her haunches had an amphibian quality, half human and half of another world. It was laborious, and yet had the simplicity and poise of a tortoise's amble; when she finished, hardly a speck remained, the floor was bright as a mirror or a lake on a calm day. Then, at last, she would unbend her body and straighten her back. Most of the time she worked, her body was slightly bent, as if in obeisance to an invisible god.

There were several ways of spending a Sunday evening. You could drive to Outram Ghat, and then stroll with your family by the River Hooghly, watching balloons floating volitionlessly in the air, the steamers in the water, the smoky outline of the Howrah Bridge, like an altar on the horizon. You could stay at home and listen to plays on the radio once the football commentary was over: comedies, melodramas, whodunits. The heroine's voice would quiver like a note on the violin; the star-crossed lovers would frequently cry 'Never!' and 'Forever!'; the murderer would murder accompanied by drums and

cymbals; the funny man would mispronounce words and fall in love with the heroine. It was like Shakespeare, and yet it was not like Shakespeare.

Sometimes Chhaya would come in and say excitedly: 'They're showing a seenema in the field!'

'Seenema! What seenema?' Mamima would ask.

'*Street-Singer*,' she would reply, or the name of some other such film made forty years ago in the New Theatres.

The boys would run up to the terrace and lean out to look at the field that lay beyond the professor's house. This surprising piece of empty land, which builders and contractors had somehow overlooked, was usually a meeting-place for fireflies; at night, wandering with their small lights, their miniature green hurricane-lamps, they turned the silent field into a lighted marketplace of activity. Servants and their children, rickshawallas, people from the basti, had now gathered in the field to watch the seenema; a great piece of white cloth had been hung between two poles at one end. After some time, giant black and white figures came alive on the piece of cloth, and a white funnel of light ran from the projector to the screen; the audience sat dwarfed by the indistinct majesty of the figures moving before them. Voices, loud and elemental as thunder, boomed from a

scratchy soundtrack. Sandeep tried to follow the story, but all he comprehended was the sound of thunder and the darkness of evening and the dance of black and white phantoms.

When they came down, their eyes smarting, Chhotomama looked up from the newspaper and said:

'Let's go for a drive.'

And Mamima, who had been sewing a button onto a trouser, bit the thread and asked:

'Where to?'

'Anywhere,' said Chhotomama, with child-like conviction.

'But won't you be tired driving? You have work tomorrow.'

'The roads will be deserted today. The roads are always deserted on Sunday.'

They went down; Chhotomama backed the car out of the small garage that was attached to the house. It was an old, grey Ambassador; its faded, mottled colour did not seem to be its natural colour, but a complexion attained with age and unrewarded industry. It was battered like an old cardboard box, and the needles on the dials on its dashboard never changed direction, like futile compasses always pointing north. When it ran, the engine and the ramshackle body of the car combined to

make a grating, earthy noise, like a drunk man cracking an obscene joke in a guttural dialect and laughing at it at the same time.

Chhotomama sat at the steering-wheel with superior confidence; Mamima and Sandeep's mother huddled in womanly league at the back; the three boys were crammed together in the front, Sandeep by the window, Abhi next to him, and Babla, inside, between his father and his brother, where it was hottest. The best place, by the open window, was graciously afforded to Sandeep by his two cousins, and Sandeep accepted it graciously, a tyrant condescending to please his subjects. Babla, the youngest, had to be content to squeeze into the worst place. It seemed there was no democracy among children—always an aristocracy based on strength, intellect and seniority. But seniority counted most, because a boy of ten is bound to be stronger and cleverer than a boy of nine, having spent an extra year in the world, at a time when each year is like a precious deposit in a newly opened bank account. Among boys of the same age, there would be a silent tussle, a clean, honourable contest. Once a leader emerged, however, no elections were held.

They went past the bridge in Dhakuria, past Gol Park, where a statue of Swami Vivekananda, with arms

folded in fierce serenity, stood staring unflinchingly at an advertisement for biscuits; past Gariahat Market; past Rashbehari Avenue, which would be lit with rows and rows of shops on a weekday, and which was distinguished by having the largest number of under-wear shops in the world; then into Chowringhee with its colonial buildings, vacant and proud, looking on Sunday evening like a black and white photograph of another era.

A swift, streamlined breeze, such as only blows on summer nights, came in through the window. Sandeep, who envied birds and fish because they could float in their chosen element, the fish by moving with the tide and the bird by opening its wings and allowing the wind to carry it, transport it, loved going for drives because it seemed to him the only human equivalent of floating, of letting one's legs rest and setting one's body adrift. As the car turned right into Park Street, he felt at peace as effortless images of shops and restaurants passed by him as coral and anemones pass by a fish's life. A sports shop—the red letters said CASTLEWOOD (INDIA)—had its glass doors closed, but its lights were on, and he could see two tennis racquets crossed diagonally behind the shop window. Still and surreal, they had the finality of a religious symbol. The car passed Flury's, teashop,

cake-shop and idler's den in one, where young clerks came with their newly married wives, wives they had never spoken to before marriage and whom they were still shy and unfamiliar with, and with whom they tried to make halting conversation across the table, where clever young men from St Xavier's College came to glance sideways at the young, unassuming wives, who glanced sideways at them, together with the Anglo-Indians and the Chinese from Free School Street—here they congregrated, like votaries belonging to a single religious order, each morning, afternoon and evening, drinking tea and eating sausage rolls and nodding at each other. Around the giant letters, FLURY'S, were sprinkled small, absurd, many-coloured stars, a parody and tender caricature of the stars of the universe. 'Mondays Closed' said a melancholy sign. As the battered car drifted homeward, the rear-window, in wide-eyed ignorance, recorded the last images—empty pavements, a drunk leaving a bar, a dog at a zebra-crosssing—of Park Street.

# 3

Monday morning came like a fever. Chhotomama would be at the dining table, eating a rapid meal of dal, fish and rice, trying to avoid chewing as much of it as possible, before he rushed to work. Then he would run upstairs, where a pair of polished black shoes would be waiting for him, like a long-promised gift. He would spend five minutes persuading his feet to enter the shoes, or the shoes to swallow his feet. When this was done, he would knot the shoelaces and stand up straight, returning the stare of the world with a look of schoolboyish triumph; in a white shirt and grey trousers, he would look like a different person. He would become an archetype of that familiar figure who is not often described in literature—the ordinary breadwinner in his moment of unlikely glory, transformed into the centre

of his universe and his home. Over and over again, he would shout, 'I'm late!' in the classic manner of the man crying 'Fire!' or 'Timber!' or 'Eureka!', while Saraswati and Mamima scuttled around him like frightened birds.

Then he would rush downstairs and start the car, which would make angry, reproachful noises. At last he would back it out of the garage and drive it down the lane, while a group of ragged urchins ran behind it cheerfully, shouting and waving their arms, looking like a school of tiny ancillary fish in the wake of a whale. Not until the last sputter of its engine had died away, and the last grey clouds of its exhaust-fumes blended with the atmosphere, did peace reign once more resignedly over the household. These mornings would have been intolerable if they had not possessed the ring and obstinate fanfare of a Hindu festival or wedding-ceremony, which distracted everyone and kept them from thinking or analyzing too deeply; they would have been unbearable if it hadn't been known that the chaos never lasted more than twenty-five minutes.

Sometimes, late in the morning, a young man—any young man, useless and unambitious, perhaps distantly related to the family—would arrive at Chhotomama's house on his way to or from somewhere, patches of

sweat darkening his colourless shirt, a white layer of prickly-heat powder around his neck.

'Didi,' he would say to Sandeep's aunt, with excessive politeness, 'did you remind Dadabhai about my job?'

'What's the use?' Mamima would say, bringing him a glass of water. 'Does he listen to what I say? Does he have time to listen?'

'But you must remind him,' he would reply, rebuking her gently. 'Again and again and again.'

There would be an oily smile on his face, and his features and facial muscles, lubricated by a desperate, greasy willingness to please, would become extremely, marvellously, mobile. He would glance at Sandeep and whisper confidentially to Abhi:

'Who's this?'

'My cousin-brother Sandeep.'

'Sandeep . . .' he would murmur. 'Where do you live, Sandeep?'

'Bombay.'

'Bombay . . .' he would repeat, as if betrayed, a mixture of distrust and tragic reverence for the unattainable in his voice. 'Bombay is a nice city . . .' He would pause. 'Though some prefer Calcutta.' He would pause again. 'Calcutta has charm.' With every pause, this perspiring, jobless man would grow smaller and smaller on the

21

divan, and Sandeep bigger and bigger, like a trick of animation in a cat and mouse cartoon.

After another thoughtful pause, he would ask, as if this would decide everything:

'Do you play football?'

'No,' Sandeep would say.

Abashed and hurt, but trying to recover, he would ask:

'What will you be when you grow up?'

It was Sandeep's turn to hesitate, and he would say:

'A writer.'

'A *writer?*'

'He writes in English,' Abhi would reveal.

Once more, the man would diminish and Sandeep grow several feet in this endless, terrifying cartoon.

'*English?* And what will you write when you grow up?'

'Horror stories.'

The man would become more relaxed now, and ask patronizingly:

'Oh horror stories . . . How old are you?'

'Ten.'

'How many brothers do you have?'

'None.'

'How many sisters, then?'

'None.'

*'None?'*

It would go on like this for some time. The man did not seem to like Sandeep, which was a pity, because Sandeep liked the man.

In the evenings, people came out on the balconies in the lane: widows in white saris, housewives with children in their arms. The men returned home, slowly. Sandeep and his cousins sat on cane stools on the verandah, watching the balconies on the opposite side, each with its own characters, its own episodes.

In a house further down the lane, three sisters leaned against the railings in freshly pressed saris, one holding a bamboo fan. They murmured to each other and covered their mouths with their hands when they laughed. They were known as Cinderella's Ugly Sisters, but the analogy ended there, because there was no Cinderella in the family. Disappointingly, the ugly sisters were not even ugly. But they were more than twenty-five years old, and still unmarried, which is why people had begun to think there was something physically wrong with them. No woman above twenty-five and single at the same time was beautiful.

A teacher and his wife lived in the house exactly opposite. They had a twelve-year-old son whom Sandeep

and his cousins disliked because he always came first in class, and batted and bowled at cricket matches. He belonged to that despicable species called the 'all-rounder'. His father wanted him to be a success in life: a manager in a large company, perhaps. Everywhere in the lane, fathers prayed their sons would be successes. One would be a doctor because his father had once wanted to be doctor. Another would be an engineer. Another would go to America and be a famous scientist. No effort would be spared; 'future' and 'career' had become Bengali words, incorporated unconsciously but feverishly into daily Bengali parlance.

The teacher also had a ten-year-old daughter, who was being taught how to dance and paint and sing, besides how to talk and read and write, so that, when she was twenty-one, she could be married to a success in life: a manager in a large company, perhaps. The urge to do well, which existed behind closed windows like libido, was sad and strangely obscene, because no one would admit to it. Meanwhile, children, like Egyptian slaves, dragged huge blocks of frustrating study all day to build that impressive but non-existent pyramid of success.

On certain evenings, when Chhotomama was home, he would call out across the lane to the teacher's ten-year-old daughter:

'Chandrima, give us a dance!'

The girl, standing on the balcony with both her hands on the railings, and her face resting on her hands, would shake her head elaborately from side to side. She would open her lips to print a silent 'No' on the air, and dangle her body shyly. So Sandeep's uncle and his aunt would both cry out:

'Come on Chandrima, give us a dance. You know we love your dancing!'

After some coaxing and persuasion, Chandrima would begin to dance on the balcony, and the balcony would become a stage. She would embroider funny gestures with her small hands, so that they looked now like an absurd bird, and now like a doe's head, and now like barely visible wings. All the time, she would be singing to herself and swaying from side to side, beating a rhythm on the floor with her foot, and never managing to do it in perfect measure. Scornfully, Sandeep looked away, talking to his cousins; yet he could not resist glancing, too frequently, at that swaying figure from the corner of his eyes. When the performance was over, the girl ran inside with a sharp, involuntary shyness, while Chhotomama shouted, 'Wonderful! Amazing!'; for some reason, Sandeep's heart shouted within him, but he did not say a word.

Untidy but regular activity continued on the pavement. Girls played hopscotch; three boys sat on the ground, shooting marbles; a child was practising how to walk—each time it took a careful, tentative step forward, a step taken with huge, melodramatic conviction, its other leg forgot it was a leg, and the child, bewildered by its own body, collapsed in a soft heap. It began to cry and its tears made its elder sister smile; stooping, she lifted it with thin, lovely arms.

With a loaded tray in her hands, Sandeep's aunt came into the verandah. There were cups of tea on the tray, and three tumblers of milk for the boys. There was also a small, earthen pot with dark, fried sweetmeats, each an orb, dipped in syrup.

She set the tray on the floor of the verandah, which had just been swept clean by Chhaya; then she bent her knees, slowly lowering her body, and sat down on the floor herself. She was most comfortable on the newly cleaned floor, her bright red and blue sari thickening around her, crumpling into several folds, her hands moving carefully through the minor storm of her garments as she served the sweetmeats. Her legs, like two romantic, indefinite paths on a mountainside, were lost in her sari's vast landscape.

# 4

Later, when they came inside, Sandeep found his uncle sitting with a friend at the dining table. They were talking enthusiastically about something, and banging their fists on the table, making one or two old pots tremble—the table was used as much for banging (a kind of drum-roll to indicate the significance of what was being said) as it was for eating. It was old and weathered; stains from tea-cups and gravies and dirty fingers had multiplied on it like signatures. But it was clean; each afternoon, each night, Saraswati wiped it with a wet, dirty-looking rag, which, in spite of its appearance, was actually clean too, clean like the soul of a wronged criminal.

In the kitchen, Sandeep's aunt had gathered black 'jaams' onto a plate. Every May, around this time, 'jaams'

came into the markets and houses of Calcutta, dark and shiny as grapes or berries. His aunt put them into a small pan, added mustard-oil and sugar, and then put the lid on. Solemnly but fiercely, she began to shake the pan up and down, holding it tightly in her hands.

'Now,' she said between clenched teeth, her voice shaking with her shaking body, 'now we turn the "jaam" into pulp, and mix it thoroughly with the mustard-oil and sugar.' She sounded like a woman on a cooking programme on radio. Politely, Sandeep enquired if he could have the opportunity of shaking the pan. With his aunt's permission, he took it in his hands and shook it vigorously, a mildly spiteful expression on his face. No mercy, no restraint was to be shown towards the 'jaam'. One by one, they took turns—his aunt, Sandeep, Abhi, even Babla—abandoning their civilized facades and letting themselves go the moment they held the pan, like prophets on the verge of a vision or epileptics surrendering to a seizure. In the end, the 'jaam' became soft and moist and pulpy, purplish in colour, both sweet and tangy, delicious.

It was served in bowls to Chhotomama and his friend, who ate the rich, battered flesh and spat out the thick seeds after sucking them dry onto a platter. Sandeep sat down casually at the table. He liked listening

to his uncle talk about business. He liked it because his uncle's account of the small-business world always seemed like a suspense-story or a myth or a fairy-tale, full of evocative characters that worked themselves slowly into his imagination: cheats, sophisticated two-timers, astringent moralists, clever strategists, heroic fighters, risk-takers and explorers. Each new business venture sounded like a new military onslaught, each new product like a never-before weapon capable of conquering the world added to a nameless arsenal. And Sandeep believed every word of it, that is, the tone of the words rather than the words themselves, because they were said with such confidence, such superior conviction. Only the other grown-ups seemed unpardonably cynical about Chhotomama's abilities. They said things like: 'Anindo doesn't have a head for business. If he'd stuck to a proper job, he would be leading a better life.'

But the children had boundless faith in him. Abhi had told Sandeep that the latest machine his father's factory had made was an agricultural device that could gather rice from the fields, separate the chaff from the grain, and then bundle it, all at once.

'It's the only one of its kind in the world,' Abhi said gravely. Sandeep nodded, equally grave, and wondered

about this magical implement, this work of genius. Surely this amazing machine should have silenced all the grown-ups? Were they jealous? Though, granted, Chhotomama had led an unpredictable life. When he had been a student, he had believed he was a communist, and had planned his part in the coming revolution with great passion and earnestness. History would take care of everything; no more would the square pegs have to be fitted into round holes and the round pegs into square ones. When the coming revolution failed to come, he had begun to believe he was a businessman, and had invested all his savings, with a few friends, into starting a small company. He still had that passionate temperament, and he now planned his new transactions and ventures with the involved enthusiasm with which he had once planned revolutions. Whenever he had doubts, his friends convinced him not to have any, and he agreed with the air of a man who enjoys being convinced. There were times when it seemed a wonderful 'pretend' game, not real or dangerous at all, like the games Sandeep and Abhi played in the afternoons. Figures of expected earnings—half a million, one million, two million—expanded and contracted in the air, the endless zeros rose and burst like balloons, the huge sums were lost in an imaginary world of numbers . . .

It was unbearably hot the next afternoon. The sun had come closer to the earth; the hours seemed trapped in an unending midday. Exhausted, they took frantic baths, the children drenching each other in a circus of water, and then they sat, their blue-black hair combed and shining beneath the dervishing fan.

Shonamama rang the doorbell. He was a bachelor, Sandeep's mother's eldest brother, and he lived a twenty-minute bus-ride away from Chhotomama's house. A pensioner, he walked through the lanes of Calcutta with a black umbrella in his hand which threw a dark island of shadow around him. Now he climbed up the staircase slowly, enjoying the shadows and the cold touch of the bannister on his hand. The stone stairs seemed to exhale a coolness as the roads outside radiated trembling, enervating gasps of heat. Entering the room, he closed his black umbrella delicately, and called out:

'Saraswati, a glass of cold water.' Then, turning to the boys, 'Now we *really* know that the Tropic of Cancer runs through Calcutta.'

'Does it really?' asked Sandeep. 'Does it really, Shonamama?'

'Of course it does,' he said peremptorily, and proceeded to drink the cold water from the glass in a single draught, pausing neither for breath or thought.

31

He made a strange gurgling sound as he drank, and his Adam's apple bobbed up and down. The glass had been covered on all sides in a cold, vapoury sweat, a fine, chilled dew trickling from top to bottom, and Sandeep brushed his fingers against it, and taking the dew, smeared its moisture on his forehead and his neck.

'Aaaah,' said Sandeep and Shonamama at the same time.

They had shut all the windows and closed the shutters so that the room was a large box covered by a lid, cool and dark and spacious inside. And they were like tiny insects living in the darkness of the box, breathing in the air of the world through invisible perforations. Whenever there was a power cut, they fanned themselves meditatively with newspapers or bamboo fans, and the children deserted the bed and lay down or sat down on the floor, because the floor was a stone slab of coolness, an expanse of warm ice that would not melt. Sandeep's aunt and mother lay on the bed, murmuring to each other, and each time they turned, there was a shy and subtle clink of bangles. And whenever the power returned, the fan whirred at full speed, and the silent room filled with its gentle, understated hum. Shonamama was sitting on the stool in the far side of

the room, reading a book by the light of a single lamp. It seemed strange, that lamp shining in the daytime, and the room so dark, as if night had fallen inside it.

Sometimes, Sandeep and Abhi would walk up quietly to a window and open a single shutter, slanting it so that as little light entered the room as possible. Then they both peered through it; it was like peering into the narrow slit of a letter-box. They were momentarily blinded; outside, everything dazzled intolerably; a few people walked on the pavement like survivors, vanquished by the heat. It was possible, on certain moments, for Abhi and Sandeep to call out to a dazed passer-by, 'Eh, stupid!' or 'Faster, fat man!' and close the shutter and become invisible. Then they would break into loud hiccups of laughter; they felt they had the dangerous power to unsettle the world outside, and then fade innocently into thin air, like spirits. The heat outside and the coolness inside made them feel inviolable and reckless.

Once or twice, Sandeep remembered Bombay and felt oddly unhappy without knowing why. Alone in the big apartment on the twenty-third floor, he was like Adam in charge of paradise, given dominion over the birds and fishes; he was too much in the foreground. He hated being in the foreground; he wanted a housefly's anonymity. At school, he was Adam expelled, at large

among the alien and the unforgiving. But here, in Chhotomama's house, he pulsed into life and passed into extinction according to his choice; he had liberty.

During these alternating bouts of happiness and unhappiness, when Sandeep felt his equilibrium disturbed, his thoughts would run something like this: 'I wish it were the first day of the holidays, and I had just come back from school, and I had just entered my room, and I had just heard we were going to Calcutta.' His mind went back to that moment, which had never really existed in quite that way, and savoured it.

To regain his composure, all he had to do was take a second look through the shutter. A bhelpuri vendor was wandering past, his prop under his arm, the basket of bhelpuri balanced almost stylishly, like a Malaysian fedora, on his head. Later, the key-man went by, with a cluster of keys around a large ring, the metal shimmering against the sun, the keys jangling. The vendor had called out in a loud voice, *'Bhelpuri!'*, but the key-man had said nothing; he had simply shaken the ring and let the jangling keys speak for him. The strange metallic whisper of the keys could be heard, immaterial and ghostly, even when the man had disappeared, seemingly evaporated by the heat.

# 5

Sandeep woke in the sharp light of morning to shouts coming vague and muffled from the distance. He rubbed his eyes, knelt upon the pillow, then jumped sideways from the bed to the window. His cousins were already there, watching something with deep patience and interest. It was their father. He was late as usual. He was sitting at the steering-wheel of the old Ambassador, one arm casually hanging outside, one arm on the wheel, glancing backwards enquiringly, as if he were checking some crucial point no one else could see. A few idle men had gathered around the decrepit car.

'Okay boys, start pushing,' Chhotomama commanded without turning his head, looking keenly at a private landmark on the horizon.

The idlers were quite unexpectedly altered into purposeful, energetic men, as if someone had turned a key in their backs. They took position, like a small battalion—two by the window, two at the back, and another reserve, who would do the indispensible work of shouting from the rear. At Chhotomama's words, the team strained forward, and the recalcitrant car, after some stolid silent thought, decided to concede a few feet into the road. People had come out on the balconies, and were watching with sympathetic curiosity. Their eyes followed the car's reluctant progress; their lips parted to pass a few well-considered comments; husbands and wives who had quarrelled the previous night were reunited in their avid appreciation of the spectacle; brothers who could never agree about a single point reached a brief consensus about the condition of the vehicle; astonished children who had never spoken anything but thickly meditative nonsense uttered, to the delight of their mothers, their first word as the car belched twice into motion and then stopped again.

Sandeep and his cousins stared out in embarrassed silence. As they watched, their heads turned together in exactly the same way; tilted at an identical angle; their necks craned with painful tension as the disgruntled car moved beyond view. There was an apprehensive hush,

then a faint rumble, then excitement as they saw the car returning, this time facing the other side of the road.

'Harder, boys, harder!' persuaded his uncle.

He looked almost heroic and serene, in complete control of the troubled situation. Sandeep's aunt, who had been in the verandah on the first storey, surreptitiously entered the room. She glanced shyly out of the window, then turned away, covering her eyes.

'Why don't we stick to horse-carriages?' she whispered.

Chhotomama had passed out of view again. Sandeep tried to insinuate his head between the gaps of the mullions, but failed. Then there was a sudden throbbing in the distance, culminating in a long drawn-out roar, an affirmative crescendo at the end of a tiresome musical. The engine had come to life. The five men returned, sweating, talking loudly and rapidly, showing off, playing to the gallery.

'Boudi!' they called. 'Boudi!'

'Yes?' said Sandeep's aunt, hesitantly approaching the window.

'We sent Dada off, finally!' announced the reserve, who had shouted the most because he was gifted with an impressive voice. 'The car's all right!'

Sandeep's aunt nodded and smiled. She knew that this kind of thing occurred too frequently in

the mornings, and the derelict, geriatric car changed into a difficult, obstinate animal. It was one of those beasts that the people of Calcutta had been unable to domesticate—better, perhaps, to go back to the horse and the horse-carriage. On bad days like this, when the fans stopped turning because of a power-cut, when the telephone went dead because of a cable-fault, when the taps became dry because there was no power to pump the water, and finally, when the car engine curtly refused to start, it seemed a better idea to return to a primitive, unpretentious means of subsistence—to buy a horse and a plough, to dig a well in one's backyard, to plant one's own trees and grow one's own fruit and vegetables. Calcutta, in spite of its fetid industrialization, was really part of that primitive, terracotta landscape of Bengal, Tagore's and the wandering Vaishnav poet's Bengal—the Bengal of the bullock-cart and the earthen lamp. It had pretended to be otherwise, but now it had grown old and was returning to that original darkness: in time, people would forget that electricity had ever existed, and earthen lamps would burn again in the houses.

There were two rooms on the second and topmost storey. The first was the large one facing the road; here, Sandeep and his cousins slept and woke, and here they wrote and

rewrote themselves into their imaginary expeditions and adventures. There were two beds, one big and one small, on which they voyaged daily into nowhere. The cupboards rose like ugly reefs from a fictional ocean, casting long, rectangular shadows in the evening. At one end of the room, there was a mirror and a dressing-table; the mirror imaged the room and gave it a sense of extra space. Next to it, there was a wooden clothes-horse, with several horizontal bars running parallel to, and on top of, each other. One would have expected to find it in a gymnasium, but here it was—it was called an alna, and all kinds of clothes and garments hung from its ribs. A lizard lived behind it.

The other room, facing the backyard, a few palm trees, a field and a professor's house, was much smaller, with one double bed in it. Near the window, there was an ungainly study-table, with Abhi's textbooks on it, and metal boxes that contained pencils, rulers and erasers. But no one who studied at this table would ever read more than a page because, just by the open window, almost at arm's length, was a palm tree wearing its rings of coconuts like jewellery, balancing a crow on its broad, fan-tail leaf, and behind the palm tree was the professor's house, with two daughters always getting in each other's way, a rooster, an educated-looking dog

and a cat without a conscience, and the professor's son, who performed such enviably intricate exercises in the morning. You just had to watch that window.

Within this room there was another room, hidden away in the corner. Three steps rose to it; it was a world within a world; a world, in fact, more richly inhabited than the sparse outer husk in which it was enclosed. If you sat at the study-table, it was just on your left. It was the prayer-room. Different gods and goddesses reclined or stood in various postures within. Krishna was there with his flute, his peacock-plume, and his mildly flirtatious smile; Saraswati sat thoughtfully upon her swan, playing her veena endlessly and attentively; Lakshmi was accompanied by her mascot, the white owl; Ganesh, with his humorous elephant-head, had been afforded a place as well, with his unlikely mascot, the giant rodent. Durga, the mother-goddess, had been given a slightly more prominent place than the rest. Elegant and self-contained, she rode a fierce lion. Of all the gods, Sandeep liked Ganesh the best, because he seemed so content with his own appearance.

After her bath, Sandeep's aunt would wrap a sari around herself, not wearing the blouse as yet, so that her bare shoulders showed above the borders of her sari, gleaming, a little moist. She would not approach the

gods until she had bathed; then she must rub Jabakusum oil vigorously into her hair, till the black hair reflected the sunlight, and turned almost silvery. It was a sweet-smelling oil, dark-red and rich, like wine.

She entered the prayer-room and lit two incense sticks, then stuck them, like slim pencils, into a perforated brass stand. She arranged slices of cucumber and oranges and sweet white batashas on three brass plates and placed them in front of the gods. The gods too are hungry, she said, They too need nourishment. Sandeep smiled politely but contemptuously when he heard this. But when do they eat? he enquired patiently. She muttered something incoherently—not an answer, but a mantra she had begun to repeat to herself as soon as she sat upon the shatranji on the floor.

Sometimes it was a mantra; sometimes it was a long incantation about the exploits of a god or a goddess—how, for instance, a demon had been outwitted, or a demon's sister been embarrassed. Or it was a description of a divine wedding; how a god had won an earthmaiden, or how a goddess had been won by a mortal king after a prolonged and wasteful courtship. They were an irresponsible lot, jealous of each other, doing silly, petty things at times and silly, spectacular things at others—not unlike Sandeep and his cousins.

Sandeep himself did not believe in God, much less in gods. Like most children, he was the opposite of innocent: he was sceptical but tolerant of other creeds. What he enjoyed about the act of worship had little to do with belief or disbelief in divinity; it was the smell of sandalwood incense, the low hum of his aunt's voice, the bell ringing at the end of the ceremony, the white batashas, clean as washed pebbles, taken out of a bottle hidden in a small cupboard, the cool taste of the offerings that were distributed after the prayer, in fact, the general, dignified uselessness of the whole enterprise. And he liked the sight of his aunt surrounded by her gods in that tiny room, like a child in a great doll-house, blowing the conch eloquently; it was a strange sight, to watch a grown-up at play. Prayer-time was when adults became children again.

At lunchtime, at the dining-table, Sandeep asked his aunt:

'Mamima, what did you pray for today?

Separating some tiny and particularly persistent bones from the fish, she replied:

'Oh, I prayed the car would start in the mornings.'

'Didn't you pray for a new car?' asked Abhi, a high-pitched inflection of disappointment in his voice.

They went on eating, inspecting the fish, searching for the fishbones, the tiny, tiny fishbones. Babla sat with his mouth open, into which his mother put little balls of fish and rice. What you prayed for mattered least in the prayer-room; all that mattered was the vivid entertainment of the instant. The gods, in their supreme, all-seeing inadvertence, forgot to answer the prayers, and the devotees didn't care. All that was important to the gods and the mortals was the creation of that rich and endlessly diverting moment in the small chamber, that moment of secret, almost illicit, communion, when both the one who prayed and the one who was prayed to were released from the irksome responsibility of the world. Oranges, white batashas, cucumbers.

# 6

In the morning, the sweeper came equipped with brooms and rags to wash the toilets and the bathrooms. He was tall and ugly, and his eyes were always bloodshot. He had an angry look about him, but he wasn't an angry person at all; simply a dirty and a surprisingly clumsy one. He made an awful noise as he worked, banging things here and there; perhaps it soothed his nerves in some way. The only time he usually spoke was at the end of the month, when he demanded, in a loud, half-joking voice, as if he were amused at something, his wages.

He had a son who accompanied him at times, who was around thirteen years old. He had stopped going to school four years ago, and had begun to help his father. When he came to Chhotomama's house, he carried a bucket half-full of water in one hand and a rag in the

other, with a mixture of aplomb and hesitation that reminded Sandeep of a soldier crossing a minefield. He was called Nimai, after the wandering, saffron-clothed saint who preached love to the people of Bengal. The sweeper was a religious man, and, deep down, he believed in the all-pervasive power of love.

One morning, the sweeper came to give his excuse for not having turned up to clean the toilets the last two days. He had brought his excuse with him. It was a baby, its face a fist, its eyes crinkled, and when a hand brushed the tiny strip of cloth that covered it, its naked thighs and buttocks were revealed, and also, in a flash of humorous candour, the fact that its sex was female.

'It's only two days old,' he said with some surprise in his voice, as if he were taken aback each time he tried to understand it. Nimai, meanwhile, was distributing dry, yellow sweets from a cardboard box, an important smile on his face.

'We thought *she* would die this time, it was so difficult,' said the sweeper, tenderly emphasizing the pronoun that referred to his wife. 'Nothing bad happened, thank God.' He smiled broadly, revealing bad teeth. 'Anyway, it's got *her* complexion.' The baby was dark as a tree-trunk. 'Didimoni, perhaps you don't know, but it's her fourth child,' he said, as if it were not his.

45

Sandeep's mother replied severely, 'Four children are enough, Ganesh. You'll send this one to school, hopefully.'

'Oh yes!' said the sweeper, a look of great responsibility in his eyes, mingled with sly enthusiasm. 'An English-medium school I'll send this one to, Didimoni!'

'Bengali-medium or English-medium, you must stop having children now if you want to raise these three probably. Poor Nimai has already lost his chance of an education.'

Poor Nimai, still distributing sweets and eating some of them himself, did not look as if he minded unduly.

The time came when the baby was to be passed from person to person. All the three boys wanted to hold it, but there was the delicate question of weight. There is an episode in the *Ramayana* in which princes from various kingdoms file into King Janak's court and try their hand at lifting his great, ponderous bow, in order to win his virtuous and beautiful daughter, Sita. Everyone fails except Ram, who lifts the bow with a powerful flourish, and pulls the string till it resonates and breaks. Sandeep and Abhi and Babla discovered that, unfortunately, they did not have a Ram among them, and the dangerous precariousness with which they tried to hold the baby made it apparent that the baby

was far heavier for them than King Janak's bow was for Ram. What was to be done? Humiliated, with sheepish smiles on their faces, they saw the baby transported into the arms of the women. Later, it was laid on the large double bed, where it waited on its back, like a helpless tortoise on its shell, remarkably tolerant and unprotesting. There, Saraswati, the maidservant, and Chhaya, the floorcleaner, found it when they came into the room. 'The baby! Ganesh's baby!' They squeezed it into a ball. They rolled it like dough. They tossed it in the air like a bag of cottonwool. When they kissed it, they blew into it like a balloon. Chhaya leaned secretively towards it and said, 'Ablablablablabla.' Sandeep, listening, enjoyed the comically incantatory sound of baby talk. The nonsensical words recreated a world of pure elemental feeling. The syllables came out, shapeless, formless. It was a caricature of language, and the baby liked it.

In the afternoon, drugged by an alternation of soporific heat and coolness, light and shade, Sandeep's aunt and his mother fell asleep. The magazines they had been reading lay open—one on the recipe page, and one on a story of unrequited love—on their faces; there, they fluttered like wings with every exhalation of breath. A small transistor-radio lay in Sandeep's mother's hand,

vibrating eerily with music; from afar, it looked like a singing book. One could hear muted thumps from the terrace, like a heartbeat, as Saraswati washed clothes and banged them against the floor.

The boys, in a rare, unenergetic moment, were sprawled by the window, looking at pigeons. The pigeons, red eyes and rainbows around their violet-black necks, were moving about on the parapet studiously. Copulation and some scatological considerations were all that preoccupied them. The furthest extent of their aesthetic contribution to life was the intricate manner in which they arranged their excrement on the parapet, so that it came to resemble a mosaic or an abstract graphic on stone. Defecation was a purely inspirational act with them, arbitrary and spontaneous as the Romantic's conception of his poem.

At present, one pigeon in particular was entertaining himself by bullying other pigeons near him. Wheeling in mock anger, strutting up and down like a rich businessman in a small town, nodding his insufferable little head continually, making loud gurgling noises in his beautiful throat, he made himself a majestic nuisance to those around him. At first, the others ignored him politely, till a rebel pecked him critically on the head. The pigeon did not like being criticized. A fight ensued,

more sound and fury than anything else. The flap-flap-flap-crack-flap-flap-flap pattern of the pigeons' beating wings seemed to have lulled Sandeep's mother into an even deeper serenity, for she sighed with pleasure in her sleep. Midway through the fight, one of the pigeons flew off hurriedly, and the other remained, adjusting the wrinkles on his feathers. Then he flew off as well. Their companions, heads like bits of stone, appeared not to have noticed.

On the far side of the parapet, while the rest dreamed, two pigeons began to kiss each other in a solemnly painful manner, beaks locked together, heads moving up and down simultaneously as if they were trying to release themselves from the mysterious lock. It was a strange kind of passion; it was the only way birds could embrace, or come close to embracing—locking their beaks in that funny, tortured way. Finally, the male climbed on the female's back and proceeded to flap its wings in an abstracted fashion. The female waited, bending its head in a world-weary manner.

'What are they doing?' asked Babla, noting the nuances of the scene in fascination.

Sandeep did not know.

'I think they're fighting,' he said, not sure of the validity of his own superior knowledge.

49

'If they're fighting,' said Abhi, 'why doesn't the other one struggle?'

'It's lost,' said Sandeep. 'It knows it's defeated.'

The entire spectacle, from courtship to climax to possible marital bliss or discord, lasted around ten minutes. God had apparently created these birds with the sole purpose of amusing slothful boys, and probably Himself, on unpleasantly humid afternoons.

The next morning, Mamima and Sandeep's mother went shopping. They bathed early, and wore weightless saris and outsized goggles to keep the sun out from their minds. They were possessed by the curious joy of buying things, a temporary lust which left them refreshed, exhausted, later.

Mamima's midday-prayer was postponed to a later date. The gods were not fussy about punctuality; after all, they had all eternity at their disposal. The boys, forever unemployed, went with their mothers. They took a taxi to the vegetable market at Gariahat. The taxi was on the verge of collapse: only the dust and grease and grime and rust between the arthritic joints kept it from falling into a desultory heap. The driver was a Sikh; he had kept a picture of Guru Nanak by the steering-wheel; while the driver looked at the road, the Guru, with a sun-like

halo round his head, looked at the driver. Beneath the dashboard, in a place that was painted black, were a few painted flowers, now a faded yellow, and in white letters, the name of the kind-hearted bank on whose loan the taxi had been bought.

The Sikh spoke a courteous Bengali to the women, made still more courteous and comically elaborate by the fact that it was spoken in a broad Hindustani accent and according to the rules of Hindustani grammar. This gave the gentle, rounded sounds of the Bengali language a masculine open-heartedness; it even made the language smell of onions and chappatis. Flattered and impressed, Mamima and Sandeep's mother giggled like schoolgirls.

He was a garrulous man, and he spoke, in a manner both broken and eloquent, about Calcutta. He had come here as a young man about fifteen years ago. He had first caught a glimpse of Calcutta in a black-and-white film called *Pyaasa*: it was the quay-scene showing the barges on the River Hooghly that he liked best, he said. He spoke of Calcutta with a mixture of disgust and reverence. But he no longer wanted to return to Punjab. The city, or the idea of the city given to him years ago by the black-and-white film, had absorbed him without his ever knowing it.

They got off at the market. Walking in through a

deceptively simple doorway, they found themselves wading through the beginning of an ocean of vegetables. On parallel rows of raised platforms, the vendors sat and harangued and cajoled and lovingly seduced the customers who passed critically through the little lanes in between. The ground was strewn with soiled cabbage leaves, which cats nibbled at. On the wall behind the vendors were pinned pictures of gods and goddesses from calendar-cuttings or cheap prints. Incense sticks burned before them, filling odd corners of the market with transcendental smells of sandalwood. Near the pictures of the gods were large glossy photos and posters of film-stars and cricketers, neither wholly mortal nor wholly divine. The eye rested on no empty spaces: wherever one gazed, there was a fruit, or a vegetable, or a basket, or a dog, or a god. Tiresome, fat ladies stood haggling with the vendors, stolid and immovable as pillars. One could spot a haggle from a distance: the customer and the vendor preaching endlessly to each other, like two devout and convinced priests on Judgement Day, one a mullah and the other a clergyman, trying to convert the other to his religion. The market echoed with questions and replies; fingers slyly tested the smoothness and coolness of a tomato, or the exact shade of purple of an aubergine.

One assertion was repeated like a mantra through the whole market: 'Yes sir, they're fresh. No question about it, they're fresh. See for yourself, brother, touch it, it's fresh.'

The vendors' children had turned the market's alternation of raised platforms into a playground. Between these platforms, they played hide-and-seek and lost and found and lost and found each other. Sandeep watched them from the sidelines. Two boys used an old, blighted onion for a ball, and a discarded brown-paper bag was turned into a mask. Near them, a girl of about twelve or thirteen was sitting alone behind a brown hill of potatoes. Her dress was dirty, and she had an unclean look about her; she was evidently not selling the potatoes, and, in fact, had nothing to do with the business of selling whatsoever. But she sat there, this cross-eyed girl, the squint in her eye making her look just a little deranged. The vendors and their children ignored her. She seemed quite far away and contented, however, eating bits of raw cauliflower by herself, stalks and all—until she felt Sandeep's eyes on her, which made her self-conscious, and eat the raw pieces of cauliflower in a defiant way. Sandeep thought he was falling in love with her. Later, when his mother and aunt had finished shopping and he was leaving, he glanced back to find that

she was looking at him; he could not be sure; the squint in her eye made it difficult to be sure. At any rate, one eye was looking at him, and the other one was looking at the rest of the world.

# 7

On Sundays, the streets of Calcutta were vacant and quiet, and the shops and offices closed, looking mysterious and even a little beautiful with their doors and windows shut, such shabby, reposeful doors and windows, the large signs—DATTA BROS., K. SINGH AND SONS—reflecting the sunlight. The house would reverberate with familiar voices. Chhotomama was at home. Chhordimoni, Sandeep's great-aunt, and Shonamama, his eldest uncle, had also decided to spend the day here. If you overheard them from a distance—Sandeep's uncle, his mother, his aunt, Chhordimoni and Shonamama, all managing to speak at the top of their voices without ever making a moment of sense—you would think they were having a violent brawl, or quarrelling vehemently about the inheritance of some

tract of land which they were not prepared to share. And, indeed, they *were* engaged in an endless argument (about what, they did not know) beneath which ran a glowing undercurrent of agreement in which they silently said 'Yes' to each other.

Much of the talk concerned relatives scattered all over India and all over the world. Much of it was about money and the cost of living. Chhotomama's business ran in fits and starts, like his car. It had to be pushed before it worked; it was unreliable. There was no demand for this and no demand for that; this supplier had let him down; that partner was unscrupulous and lazy; the times were not conducive to . . . In short, money was short. 'Today the palm of my left hand's itching,' said Mamima. 'God, God, I wonder—it means I'll have to spend more money—on what, I wonder.' If the right hand itched, it meant one was going to get money—but it seldom itched, and when it did, money seldom followed. Someone was not playing the game.

The subject would switch from money to people 'who need money more than we do', and these people were usually poor relations, or, to be more accurate, poorer relations, old men and widows whose sons were too young to earn or who themselves had lost interest in working for a pittance. The second case was more

frequent among men: there seemed to be something masculine about giving up one's job and dignifying one's idle hours by speculating about existence. So they had to be helped and supported, while constantly being assured that they were not being helped and supported, to which they would reply, with different degrees of sincerity, that of course they were and how could they forget it? They were helped and supported, not necessarily because they deserved it, but because money was meant to flow from the hands of one member of the family to another.

This kind of talk, whether at the dinner-table or in the bedroom, did not become too oppressive: it was too full of metaphors, paradoxes, wise jokes and reminiscences to be so. It was, at bottom, a criticism of life. And there were unpredictable breaks, when Sandeep's mother and Mamima would begin to murmur conspiratorially about the colour of a sari. And there were unpremeditated instants when everyone would suddenly stop talking, perhaps to think, each one about something different, and there would be a gap of hushed clarity, in which a crow cawed outside. And the children would be arrested in whatever they were doing at that point of time: one swinging by the window, one lying on his stomach reading a comic, and one sitting on the ground, listening and comprehending nothing. And then they would

resume their argument, very loudly, as if they were early twentieth-century actors in some green, neglected village in Bengal, where there were no mikes and no electricity, and every actor had to bellow his speech melodramatically before the large village audience would hear and applaud what he was saying. One would have almost expected Sandeep's uncles and aunts to have been attired in the splendid, vibrant costumes that folk-artistes wore in keeping with the dramatic excessiveness of their gestures. Yet his uncles wore white pyjamas and nothing else, and the women were draped in faded, handwoven cotton saris—their bodies cool even in the cumulative heat of conversation.

Sometime during the day, probably not too late, nor too early, as on weekdays, Chhotomama would take a bowl of water and other equipment to the verandah, place them on a chair, perch himself on a stool, and shave. This was one of Sunday's simpleminded pleasures and self-indulgences: to shave at what time one pleased, and as long as one pleased, with the children nearby, watching, convincing one that a morning stubble was an amazing thing, and that the shaving instruments were holy tools, and that the act of sprinkling water on the face was somehow profound. When he would look up from the mirror, he would sense the stillness of

the street around him, the endless, enduring world of pigeons and crows, the perpetual movement of pariahs, beggars and vendors, and he would feel, simultaneously, the warmth of the sunlight and the coolness of the brush on his cheek. The boys would stand around, noting his movements the way passers-by in Calcutta break their journey to work to stare at acrobats or a monkey-show on the pavement. With curiosity and envy, they followed the determined attentiveness with which he put the cream on his brush, and then swished the lather with a flourish on his face, white and frothy, till it gained a rich uniformity that looked both ornamental and delicious, and then carefully ploughed it with his razor in primitive agricultural fashion.

Later, he would enter the toilet, armed with an ashtray, a newspaper and a pair of reading-glasses. The toilet was his study. Here, filling the room with cigarette smoke, he read the significant news of the day; he pondered on 'world affairs' and 'home affairs'; he pontificated to himself on the 'current situation' from a Marxist angle. He was a water-closet thinker.

This part of the daily ceremonies over, he would enter the bathroom to have his pre-luncheon bath, humming a small tune to himself. He would turn on the old, ineffectual shower and, suddenly elated, begin singing

aloud to himself. He had a resonant tenor voice, a voice both strong and delicate. When he sang in the bath, the notes echoed in the four enclosing walls like rays of trapped light darting this way and that in a crystal, a diamond. He usually sang old, half-remembered compositions that had been popular thirty or forty years ago in a Bengal where the radio and the wind-up gramophone were still new and incredible machines breaking the millennial silence of the towns and villages:

*Godhulir chhaya pathe*
*Je gelo chini go tare.*

Roughly translated, this meant

In the hour of cow dust, on the shadowy path,
Who passed by me? I felt I knew her.

Knocking on the bathroom door, Sandeep made a pest of himself by asking: 'Chhotomama, what does *godhuli* mean?'

Lost in the general well-being of cleansing himself, his uncle replied patiently: 'The word *go* means cow, and the word *dhuli* means dust. In the villages, evening's the time the cowherds bring the cattle home. The herd

returns, raising clouds of dust from the road. *Godhuli* is that hour of cow-dust. So it means dusk or evening.'

As Chhotomama explained, his voice emerging from behind the steady sound of water, Sandeep saw it in his mind like a film being shown from a projector—the slow-moving, indolent cows, their nostrils and their shining eyes, the faint white outline of the cowherd, the sense of the expectant village (a group of scattered huts), and the dust, yes the dust, rising unwillingly from the cows' hooves and blurring everything. The mental picture was set in the greyish-red colour of twilight. It was strange how one word could contain a world within it. Quite unexpectedly, Chhotomama now began a song by Tagore:

*Bahe nirantar ananta anandadhara.*
*Baaje ashima nabhamajhe anaadiraba.*

In an unsatisfactory translation, this meant

Endless and unbroken flows the stream of joy.
Its timeless sound resonates beneath the great sky.

It was a song of praise, a prayer-song. Sandeep did not understand a single word of it, but he thought that the

tune and especially the sound of the difficult words communicated with him in an obscure way, and he was aware that the repetitive sound of the language had mingled with the sound of the water falling in the bath, till they became one glimmering sound without meaning. Whether the bath ended first, or the song, Sandeep could not tell. A cool spell of remote, waterfall-like music was woven and broken at the same time, as if the words of the song could not endure existing a hundredth of a second after they had been uttered. Chhotomama unlocked the door noisily and came out, smiling, a towel wrapped around his loins and thighs. Pottering about for his new pyjamas and vest, he looked like the chieftain of some undiscovered, happy African tribe. His wet hair stuck out in all directions from his head, like a black, untidy porcupine. The bath, the inner temple where he had performed his last sacrosanct ritual and offered his songs for the day, was now empty and without music, except the sound of a single drop of water falling on the floor with a tone and perfect pitch of its own. Every few seconds, it seemed to repeat that exact pitch without alteration or variation.

At about six o'clock in the evening, the lights went out. The power-cuts had got more frequent with the heat, and the two servant-girls and their little brother

who had come downstairs and plopped shyly on the floor to watch the Sunday film on television had to be disappointed and sent home.

'I'm sure they'll show us a better film next Sunday,' assured Sandeep's mother.

'It's not me,' said the girl with the unwashed hair and incredibly clean hands. 'It's Syed,' nodding at the boy, who had worn an imbecilic, puzzled expression ever since the lights had gone off. 'He's never seen a film.' The girl's name was Runa. She was a Muslim janitor's daughter. Sandeep was sorry to see her leave: he had often fantasized about marrying her one day. He noticed, from the corner of his eye, how her bright and ragged body ran impulsively down the stairs, and listened to her slightly hoarse, illiterate voice calling to her brother and sister to follow. The stairs were dark, and a gulf seemed to separate her from him. Then, two minutes later, he forgot she ever existed.

Saraswati brought lanterns into the room, each with a strong, yellow yolk of flame. Then she bent to light the candles, and used the dripping wax to stick them onto chipped tea saucers.

'Doesn't Saraswati look like a witch?' whispered Sandeep to Abhi. Indeed, wavering shadows from the candle flame falling and shifting on her face gave

her ordinary features a preternatural fluidity. Her cheekbones and jaw seemed to flow and change with the changing light, as if she were shedding her old face for a new one.

'Saraswati, you look like a witch,' said Abhi.

'Be quiet, you little monsters,' she replied.

She had set down the candles in their saucers at intervals on the floor: one in the room, one in the corridor, one near the staircase. It made it look like there was a festival being celebrated, some esoteric myth in the process of being retold by symbols. As Abhi leaned forward perfunctorily to blow a candle out, and Saraswati rushed towards him—her intention, she said, was to drag him out of the room by his hair—Chhotomama called from the corridor: 'Enough mischief, boys. Come on, let's go out for a walk.'

So they went out for a walk. They went through narrow, lightless lanes, where houses that were silent but gave out smells of fish and boiled rice stood on either side of the road. There was not a single tree in sight; no breeze and no sound but the vaguely musical humming of mosquitoes. Once, an ancient taxi wheezed past, taking a short-cut through the lane into the main road, like a comic vintage car passing through a film-set showing the Twenties into the film-set of the present,

passing from black-and-white into colour. But why did these houses—for instance, that one with the tall, ornate iron gates and a watchman dozing on a stool, which gave the impression that the family had valuables locked away inside, or that other one with the small porch and the painted door, which gave the impression that whenever there was a feast or a wedding all the relatives would be invited, and there would be so many relatives that some of them, probably the young men and women, would be sitting bunched together on the cramped porch because there would be no more space inside, talking eloquently about something that didn't really require eloquence, laughing uproariously at a joke that wasn't really very funny, or this next house with an old man relaxing in his easy-chair on the verandah, fanning himself with a local Sunday newspaper, or this small, shabby house with the girl Sandeep glimpsed through a window, sitting in a bare, ill-furnished room, memorizing a text by candlelight, repeating suffixes and prefixes from a Bengali grammar over and over to herself—why did these houses seem to suggest that an infinitely interesting story might be woven around them? And yet the story would never be a satisfying one, because the writer, like Sandeep, would be too caught up in jotting down the irrelevances and digressions

that make up lives, and the life of a city, rather than a good story—till the reader would shout 'Come to the point!'—and there would be no point, except the girl memorizing the rules of grammar, the old man in the easy-chair fanning himself, and the house with the small, empty porch that was crowded, paradoxically, with many memories and possibilities. The 'real' story, with its beginning, middle and conclusion, would never be told, because it did not exist.

The road ended, and it branched off, on one side, to a larger road, and on the other side to two narrower ones that led to a great field, a maidan, with a pair of poles at either end which were supposed to be goalposts. As they came closer, they noticed that the field was full of people whom they had not been able to discern at first in the darkness: now they came slowly into focus in the moonlight, like a negative becoming clearer and clearer as it was developed in a darkroom. There were all kinds and classes of people—college boys, schoolboys, couples, unemployed men, families, hawkers, groups of girls. The clammy heat had made them leave their houses or hovels in search of a breeze. It was a strange scene because, in spite of the number of people who had congregated together, there was scarcely any noise. The shadowiness of the place made them speak in low

voices, as if they were in a theatre or auditorium where the lights had been dimmed meaningfully, and a film or a play were just about to begin. If there had been no power-cut, or if it had still been light, the maidan, needless to say, would have throbbed with its own din and activity. But the darkness had brought a strange lethargy and even peace to these otherwise highly strung men and women, and there was a perceptible sense of release, as if time was oozing by, and the world happening elsewhere.

Just as Chhotomama and the boys were preparing to join the others in the maidan, to settle on the cool grass and pull the grass out luxuriously with their fingers, the lights came back. It was a dramatic instant, like a photographer's flash going off, which recorded the people sprawled in various postures and attitudes, smiles of relief and wonder on their faces. Each day there would be a power-cut, and each day there would be the unexpected, irrational thrill when the lights returned; it was as if people would never get used to it; day after day, at that precise, privileged moment when the power-cut ended without warning as it had begun, giving off a radiance that was confusing and breathtaking, there was an uncontrollable sensation of delight, as if it were happening for the first time. With what appeared to be

an instinct for timing, the rows of fluorescent lamps glittered to life simultaneously. The effect was the opposite of blowing out candles on a birthday cake: it was as if someone had blown on a set of unlit candles, and the magic exhalation had brought a flame to every wick at once.

# 8

One Friday evening, Mamima and Sandeep's mother sat in front of the dressing-table and applied a tracing of kaajal to their eyes, a faint gloss of lipstick to their lips, a line of kumkum powder in the parting of their hair, and pressed a red kumkum dot in the centre of their foreheads. They took gold bangles out of a cupboard and slipped them onto their slender wrists (the gold did not dazzle, as gold never does, but blended with the lustre and colour of their skin), and they wore firmly pressed, shimmering saris around their bodies, like bright wrapping paper around a lozenge. They gazed into the mirror and at each other with vague, approving looks, and sometimes bent down to help each other with their hair. Like lilypads, they floated on a surface of images. They dabbed themselves with perfume; each

drop of strong perfume could spread like a rumour around the room and then the house. If Mamima or Sandeep's mother had been somewhere, you could tell by the fragrance they left behind; they became strange creatures; the house became a strange forest.

They were preparing to visit relatives—an old couple who lived far away on the southern tip of Calcutta, somewhere near the road leading out from the city. It was difficult to understand why they were fussing so much about this simple visit to these simple people, unless they were using it as a pretext or an excuse to devote their passionate ardour to themselves. Devotion—that was the word: the immemorial tradition of applying kaajal and kumkum, and other ancient cosmetics like sandalwood paste and mehndi, belonged more to the world of intricate, systematic ritual than to the world of fashion; in fact, the craftsman-like way in which the women made themselves up ('making oneself up'—the same, after all, as creating oneself) reminded one of the Bengali artisans who decorate and lay the immeasurably delicate finishing touches on their idols on the day before the festival. Looking critically into the mirror, they appraised their faces and hands with a detached aesthetic interest, as if they were someone else's face and hands waiting to be adorned from simplicity to a complexity

that was oddly, unmistakably feminine. And deep down, the women also knew that the old couple living in the darkness of the suburbs would be disappointed if it were otherwise: for them, the younger relatives dressing up with such extravagance was a form of entertainment which they would talk about for days; it would be a welcome distraction in their small, clear lives; the old lady would finger the texture of their saris and ask questions; the old man would inhale the perfume without appearing to do so and sit with a pleased expression on his face.

The car broke down once on the way. Chhotomama cursed and muttered. Later, they were caught in a traffic-jam. At one point, they halted at Ganguram's at Gol Park to buy sweetmeats and a pot of sweetened pink yoghurt for the old couple. The sweetmeats and the yoghurt came in pots of red earth. All around them, people were eating from these pots and from plates made of leaves. The pots and plates would have to be discarded, sadly, once the meal was over. (Sandeep remembered the civilization of Mohenjodaro, which he had learnt about at school; there, too, people had eaten from rudimentary but graceful utensils which they had thrown away after use.) In the car, Sandeep balanced the two pots in his hands to keep the syrup from spilling, as if they were

bombs that might explode. By the time they reached the place, it was very dark. It was off the main road; as the car turned into a narrow lane with cramped shops and rickshawallas smoking dimly incandescent beedis, lounging in the corners, they moved forward in space and backward in time simultaneously. Calcutta grew remote and unrecognizable; the city was no longer clearly demarcated from the folk-tale Bengal that surrounded it so thickly. Myths and ghosts and Bengal tigers roamed beyond an unclear boundary; the sputtering car passed a temple and a tank where buffaloes and children bathed in the daytime. The place was a little colony or village tied by a network of faint lanes; there were few electric lights to illuminate the area. One's eye got reluctantly used to moonlight, and one saw houses, each some distance away from the other, and ponds in which spores settled and multiplied, on which weed formed an almost firm, palpable surface, where the lotus rose and opened with a shy passion in the darkness. So lives multiplied and opened in the cool houses and settlements of the area, or closed and remained hidden, according to conditions and circumstances. Sandeep saw hundreds of insects in the twin funnels of the car's headlights, rushing forward in an obsessive stream, an agitated Milky Way of tiny, mindless, winged life. The place made Sandeep

remember what Shonamama had once told him: 'When we were young, the world was made of small islands of consciousness. Miles separated one village, sometimes one house, from another. Letter-writing was the only means of communication—there were no telephones. A mountain or a river formed the border to our world. Our world was small, and things loomed large and astonishing for us: you wouldn't understand.'

'Where was this?' Sandeep had asked, wondering if it were a real place, or something Shonamama had dreamt up.

'In Sylhet,' replied Shonamama. 'Sylhet is now in Bangladesh.'

'Sylhet . . .' murmured Sandeep.

'When India was one big piece, and the British ruled us. When our father died, we moved to Shillong. In Shillong,' Shonamama said, 'there are mountains and waterfalls.'

As the car moved forward with difficulty through the narrow paths, Sandeep returned to Shonamama's childhood. Nothing had changed. The headlights of the car made twin stars in the darkness.

Two boys were playing carrom on the steps of a small, painted shed which had the following words on its wall

in large, black letters: NATIONAL ASSOCIATION OF SPORTSMEN. A single table-tennis table inside the shed could be glimpsed through the window. The boys interrupted their game to give Chhotomama directions to the house in a series of sporadic, enthusiastic gestures. Oh yes, they knew the old couple. And yes, their son and daughter-in-law had arrived last night with their first child.

'Is it a girl or a boy?' asked Mamima, rolling down the window.

'A girl,' said the boy.

Mamima rolled up her window before the mosquitoes came in. The two boys vanished behind them. When they reached the house, they found that the old man was waiting on the verandah with a lantern in his hand. Moths were shuddering round and round the lantern, though the old man was oblivious to them. He had come out because he had heard the throbbing of the engine in the distance. The night had been silent except for the questioning cry of an owl and the continual orchestral sound of crickets in the bushes. The throbbing of the engine had, therefore, travelled through the silence to the old man's listening ear, and to his wife's ear, even when the car was relatively far away and beyond their range of vision. They had pondered over the sound, and

finally, he had lit the lantern and shuffled out. 'I told her,' he said, referring to his wife. 'I told her that I heard the car, I knew it was the car, I told her you were coming.'

Once they were inside, Mamima gave the pot of yoghurt and the pot of sweetmeats to the old lady. 'There was no need,' she said. 'Oh really,' she said. 'This is too much,' she insisted, with the air of one who has just received the Kohinoor diamond as a birthday present. 'Come, come, come,' said Chhotomama, with the air of someone who has just given the Kohinoor diamond as a birthday present, and refuses to be overawed by his own generosity. 'It's nothing.' It *was* nothing, of course, only Ganguram's sweets and yoghurts, but they fussed and fussed and created the illusion that it was something, something unique and untasted and unencountered.

The son and the daughter-in-law emerged shyly from the anteroom. They both stooped gently to touch Chhotomama's feet, and Sandeep's aunt's and his mother's feet, a traditional greeting and a mark of obeisance towards one's elders.

'Oh no no no,' said Chhotomama, struggling to keep the son's hand away from his feet. 'There's no need for all this.' This was half a token gesture towards modesty, and half towards the new, 'modern' India—Nehru's secular India, free of ritual and religion.

'I have not met you for two years, Dada,' said the son, struggling to get his hands near Chhotomama's toes. 'You must not stop me.' This was half a token gesture towards modesty, and half towards the old, 'traditional' India—Gandhi's India of ceremony and custom.

Sandeep, meanwhile, had come to the conclusion that the grown-ups were mad, each after his or her own fashion. Simple situations were turned into complex, dramatic ones; not until then did everyone feel important and happy. Will they never grow up? thought Sandeep irately. He glanced around him. A single blue, fluorescent tube was burning on the wall. It was not a big room. Despite its bareness, the impression it gave was of austerity rather than poverty. It made one remember that poverty meant displacement as well as lack, while austerity meant being poor in a rooted way, within a tradition and culture of sparseness, which transformed even the lack, the paucity, into a kind of being. There was a wooden table in the centre of the room and a divan on one side; there was a series of shelves, carved into the wall, that had a picture of Ramakrishna and a statuette of Shiv next to incense sticks on a stand whose sandalwood fragrance brought a faint, subconscious aura of devotion to the room; there was a book of Ramakrishna's anecdotes and parables, wedding photographs, one in

black-and-white, and one of the son and daughter-in-law, in colour, a peacock feather, and a jar of spices. In one corner, there was a money-plant in a pot, and against the wall, beneath the window which opened into the branches and sweet-smelling foliage of a mango tree, there was a harmonium, and a tanpura laid horizontally. On the floor, two cane shatranjis were rolled out to sit on. The objects in the room were numerous enough to be noticed and few enough to be counted and remembered. The short stretches of empty space in between seemed to have been deliberately created by the congruence of the walls and the balance between light and shadow. Space gave the little room its strange composure and a cool, accommodating presence.

On one of the shatranjis rested what looked like a dark bundle.

'Have you seen the baby?' asked the young man, picking the bundle up.

'Ooooh,' said the women. 'What's it called?'

'Annapurna,' said the father, his voice becoming thick with affection and pride. 'My wife chose the name.'

'It's a lovely name,' said Chhotomama.

'Anna' means 'rice' or 'food', and 'purna' means 'full' or 'complete'; joined together, the two halves give birth (just as the two parents had given birth to the child)

77

to the word 'Annapurna'—Annapurna, which means Provider of Food or Sustenance, and is one of the many names of the mother goddess, Durga.

The bundle called Annapurna stirred. She had been aroused from deep slumber, yet she smiled with toothless good humour. Maybe she didn't realize she had woken up, maybe she thought she was having yet another one of her sundry many-coloured dreams. But no, she had just urinated on her father's shirt with an engrossed look on her face. By doing so, she proclaimed her return to reality. The father grumbled as a wet patch on his shirt spread and grew larger. No one was embarrassed. How could one be embarrassed about a baby urinating? The *baby* was not embarrassed. Nor did she seem to have done it with anything but the best of intentions. Besides, there was a rumour that baby's urine is particularly innocuous, even pure, like spring water.

The man hurried inside to change his shirt, and the old man took charge of his grandchild. Smiling, they all settled down to talk. The baby proceeded to play with her grandfather's spectacles, and make critical comments about the conversation.

'Oog,' she said. 'Oog.'

She thought spectacles were made to be eaten and chewed and probably digested. When Sandeep borrowed

Chhotomama's wristwatch to reflect a miraculous dot of light on the wall, she gaped respectfully. Once, when she began to cry, Sandeep held a tumbler of water against the light, and showed her the rays of light that darted in the water like tiny fish; the baby became silent, and leaned forward peculiarly, as if she were ready to change her religion. The baby was an imbecile; she could be made to believe in anything she saw. Spittle dribbled from the side of her mouth. Great cobwebs of saliva hung from her lips. This was Annapurna, a moist, unctuous thing.

The old man began to croon in her ear in a feeble voice:

Sway, sway, swaying, a comb in your bright hair,
Now the bridegroom'll come, now he'll take you
   away . . .

Annapurna tried to move; her grandfather's arms surrounded her like the Wall of China. The spectacles fell from her nerveless fingers to her grandfather's lap; her fingers became sluggish and greedy.

The daughter-in-law and the old lady had made a dinner consisting of dal, aubergines, cottage-cheese, and two kinds of fish. There was koi fish and there was rohu fish. The baby fell asleep again. What a strange life,

thought Sandeep, sleeping and waking. The old man was still singing the rhyme in her ear. The old lady took pains to see that everyone ate well. Plates had been arranged on a small, clean table. 'You must taste the koi,' she said. 'Our bou made it.' The daughter-in-law smiled. 'Won't you eat?' asked Mamima. 'Later,' they said. They watched them eat. Sandeep fell asleep, so did Abhi and Babla. 'I'll remember this koi for many days,' said Chhotomama. The daughter-in-law had vanished, but her smile remained. Sandeep woke for a lucid moment to find he was back in Chhotomama's house, in the creased warmth of the double bed, lying next to his cousins. He had not been conscious of the homeward journey. A firefly had floated in through the window, a wandering, free light. 'What's its name?' asked someone and someone replied, 'Annapurna,' and a third voice said, 'It's a lovely name.'

# 9

On Saturday, a cool breeze surprised them. It smelled of wet earth, sodden leaves. It had rained somewhere in the villages, in groves and fields, and the breeze had travelled to this lane, bringing news of rain from the far-off place of its beginnings. They had congregated after lunch on the double bed on the second storey, when it ran its fingers down their backs, making them break out in goose-flesh. There was something erotic about the first breeze that brought the monsoons.

'Did you feel that?' asked Mamima. 'Yes,' said Sandeep's mother.

'And that smell . . .' said Chhotomama, breathing in deeply.

He had never known any smell like that of wet earth, her own sweet odour, earth-musk. The most natural and unpretentious fragrance.

A few days later, there was the first kal-baisakhi storm. A layer of grey clouds covered the sky, inverting it like a bowl, shutting out sunlight. Dead leaves and old newspapers streamed through the lane like a procession of protest-marchers. Someone cried out from a balcony. A woman's voice. 'Ratna! Ratna, come in this instant!' The wind blew silent and straight. A woman walking alone on the road was teased by the wind; the loose end of her sari, the aanchal, flew helplessly, a lost fragment of colour; it was the most beautiful movement seen on this rainy day. Crows hopped alertly. They sensed a presence, powerful and dangerous, though they could see nothing and no one. The nervous, toy-like city was set against the dignified advance of the clouds, as if two worlds were colliding. There was an end-of-the-world atmosphere. Then, lightning, sometimes a single, bright scar that flashed on a cloud's black face and was gone, and sometimes filling the grey space with light. A moment's heavy silence; then the thunder spoke—

guruguruguru.

In obedience, the leaves began to tremble, and the branches moved uniformly, disciplined as a battalion

doing exercises—Bend! Rise! Bend! Rise! And, slam! a door or a window banged shut without warning; ghosts and spirits were abroad, making mischief, distracting the servants, knocking at the windows. Only the children had time to investigate or smile at the spirits, because the grown-ups were busy, panicky. Saraswati bundled the clothes left to dry on the terrace, and brought them in before they got wet—with the wrinkled clothes in her arms, she looked like Mother Teresa carrying the light, wispy bodies of dying children. Mamima rushed to shut the windows, which were banging their wooden heads in a religious frenzy. She just managed to lock the last one in time. As if by common consent, it began to rain with a steady sibilant sound. They sat in the room with the windows closed, listening to the sound of the rain beating against the windows and falling on the tin roof of the next house. The children talked to each other, but sometimes they stopped and became attentive, listening, for no apparent reason, to that sound. The room became cool; the beds and floors became cool. When they opened the taps, the water sparkled. They rinsed their mouths with the water. Sometimes, Sandeep and Abhi opened a shutter and stared out into a world where arrows of rain fell continually. They stretched out their hands. They allowed the round, orb-like raindrops

to settle on the back of their hands like dewy insects, though the drops lost shape as soon as they touched the flesh. Running to the smaller room at the back, Sandeep glanced out of the window and saw the palm tree dancing by itself, to itself. A silent wave of delight passed over him as he watched it dance.

So another season had come. In another corner of the world lay the great continent called Australia, an immense unwieldy mass of land floating on the ocean like a giant makeshift raft on water. Who had been set afloat on that raft? Kangaroos, aborigines and cricketers. And India was touring Australia, and there was a test-match being played between the two teams at Sydney. So Chhotomama would wake up at five o'clock in the morning and try to catch Sydney on the radio. He would spin the rapid knobs, and after an incoherent period of time, when the radio cackled in an evil witch-like way, the voice of the Australian commentator would come through, loud and urgent one moment, weak and distant the other, as if a few words were being carried off, on their passage towards India, by a cormorant crossing the ocean.

The room would echo with a strange Australian accent, and an odd and vivid pronunciation of vowels.

Everyone would be sleeping, of course; muffled heads and breathing bundles of bodies, because the rains had made the nights cool and relaxed. Abhi, Babla and Sandeep slept like primeval creatures huddled on the island of the bed, close to the horizon, outwaiting the dawn that would bring the first thought to their heads. Their bodies slept with a pure detached love for every moment of sleep.

Into the midst of this delicate surface world of slumber, which could be burst like a bubble so easily, and yet miraculously escaped being burst for around eight hours, Chhotomama trod heavily at five o'clock in the morning.

Twiddling the radio knobs, fiddling with this, dislodging that, coughing, laughing, yawning, he disgusted everyone with his obstreperousness, his clumsiness. The amazing thing was, *he* did not think he was making any noise; he thought that as long as he did not actually utter a word, he disturbed no one. Whatever mischief his hands and legs did, as far as he was concerned, was not his responsibility. Anyway, Sandeep and Abhi had decided that one had to simply and unquestioningly tolerate the grown-ups. One had constantly to see the comic aspects of their characters to remain sane.

The test-match came to an end. India did the one honourable thing: it lost. How could Gandhi's country bear to win? With the test-match, the sense of expectation died out temporarily. For a few days, the rains fell heavily—continuous white screens blotted out landscapes and landmarks: the main road with its tramlines, its lamp posts, its old medicine shop, and then the park; these melted before Sandeep's eyes, while he watched, a little amazed that he too did not melt away.

The gutters in the lane overflowed with an odd, languid grace. Water filled the lane; rose from ankle-deep to knee-deep. Insects swam in circles. Urchins splashed about haphazardly, while Saraswati returned from market with a shopping-bag in her hands; insects swam away to avoid this clumsy giant. Her wet footprints printing the floor of the house were as rich with possibility as the first footprint Crusoe found on his island.

Chhotomama had not gone to work; his car had failed him. The car usually became temperamental during the monsoons. It was also temperamental in the winter and the spring and the summer, but Chhotomama said it was especially temperamental in the monsoons. He did not blame the car, he blamed its maker, whoever he was.

He did some work at home, rummaging through

files. Then he scanned the newspaper, *The Statesman*, reading the editorial four times, shaking his head and laughing abrasively. 'The man is a fool,' he said quietly. 'I must write to the paper . . .' He took a foolscap sheet and began to write. He scribbled 'Dear Sir', and paused and then crossed out 'Dear'. The letter began 'Sir . . .' He was very angry with the editor.

After the letter was written, he relaxed on the bed, lying on his stomach. Whenever he relaxed, he remembered he had a terrible backache.

'Abhi!' he called. 'Come and press my back.'

Abhi came and put his fingers, gentle as a faith-healer's, on his father's vertebrae.

'Oooh . . . oooh . . .' said Chhotomama, a noise like a wind blowing through an aperture. It conveyed, at once, pain and pleasure.

'A little above,' he said, navigating Abhi's fingers.

The fingers moved a little above.

'A little—a fraction—to the left.'

The fingers shifted a fraction to the left.

'Another fraction left.'

Another fraction.

Searching for that exact spot of pain was a delicate matter, a life or several lives might depend on it; it was like trying to detect a mine in a minefield, or a vein of

oil in a desert.

'Yes, yes!' said Chhotomama. '*There*. Press it *there*.'

'Baba . . .' said Abhi, his fingers poised, a master-pianist about to embark on the opening phrase of his sonata, while the audience waits, breathless.

'*Press!*' said Chhotomama, drowning, his voice a choked bubble. 'Oh *what* is it, Abhi?'

'Baba, the cricket bat we had talked about . . .'

'It's yours,' cried Chhotomama, giving in to blackmail and letting the world know about it. 'It's yours! Now press *there*.'

Smiling, Abhi began to play his sonata. The notes rose, lovely and exultant. Chhotomama closed his eyes and sighed, intoxicated by music no one else could hear.

Fifteen minutes later, Chhotomama asked Babla to stand on his back. He was small and would be able to balance himself; he was light enough to stamp out the pain without hurting him.

'I'll fall, Baba,' said Babla, who was not a brave boy.

'Of course you won't,' said Chhotomama. 'Come, only for a few minutes.'

Babla climbed on the bed. He put one leg on his father's back. It was like the picture of Edmund Hillary on Mount Everest. All that was needed was a flag. Then

he put both his feet on his father's back.

'Walk,' said Chhotomama. 'Stay in the same place, but walk.'

It was a contradictory demand. Babla tried it. He smiled; he seemed to like the idea of staying in one place and walking at the same time. He did not know legs could do such things. It looked like the reverse of the Shiv Tandav. (The Shiv Tandav: in the last phase of the universe, when the world is old and corrupt, Shiv wakes from his trance, and sets about destroying everything. With giant strides, he stamps out life. This is the Tandav, the terrifiying, cosmological dance of destruction. The sculptors traditionally represent this with Shiv dancing, arms gracefully apart, one leg raised, the other foot on a helpless child lying on his stomach: the latter probably symbolizes the innocent life which is crushed as a part of the dance. And the Shiv Tandav was reversed when Babla, the child, danced on Chhotomama's back, while the latter lay on his stomach and made noises.)

Mamima was about to enter a competition held by a famous coffee-making company. She was filling out the entry form with an intent face. 'Mona,' she said to Sandeep, 'give me a good English slogan about coffee.' Sandeep, the boy from Bombay, who wrote poems and

stories, was supposed to have a good vocabulary in this idiotic foreign language which no one, especially coffee companies, could apparently do without. Already, he used words like 'tentative' and 'gingerly' and 'enthusiastic'. Would he help his aunt, whose command over English was imperfect, and who cared little about this, with a dignified nonchalance some Indian women have, would he help her win two air-tickets to Kashmir? 'I'll think about it, Mamima,' he said indifferently. Yet he was moved, watching her on the bed, hunched and cutting out the entry-coupon meticulously with her scissors.

Till it was lunchtime, the boys played their energetic 'pretend' games. It was good that it was raining, because they discovered they had stopped sweating. Chhotomama, out of bed, found them in the corridor.

'What are you playing?' he asked, smiling indulgently.

'We're playing freedom-fighters,' said Abhi. 'We're killing the British. We're cutting the British to pieces.'

'And who are you?' asked Chhotomama tenderly, bending low to Babla. 'Are you cutting the British to pieces as well?'

'I'm Subhas Chandra Bose,' said Babla, standing at attention and looking undauntedly into his father's eyes.

'No, I'm Subhas Chandra Bose,' said Abhi. 'Babla, shut up.'

'Abhi, shut up,' replied Babla, still at attention.

'What did you say?' asked Abhi in a mafioso voice. 'Repeat that.'

'And you?' Chhotomama asked, turning finally to Sandeep. 'Who are you?'

'I'm Mahatma Gandhi,' he said, and realized he had made a mistake.

Chhotomama was taken aback momentarily. A contemptuous smile asserted itself on his face.

'Gandhi! Gandhi was no freedom-fighter! He was a sham yogi who knew no economics!'

Sandeep did not know what 'economics' meant; he knew that the girls in his school had a class called Home Economics. 'He's the Father of the Nation,' he replied naively, repeating what he had learnt at school; he saw that, once more, he had committed an error.

Eyes burning, Chhotomama began to lecture them on pre-Independence Indian history, quoting several historians of several nationalities. As he spoke to the children, he behaved like a scholar at a seminar addressing a group of inimical scholars who had views hostile to his own. By a magical suspension of disbelief, he forgot he was talking to Sandeep and Abhi and Babla;

he saw, in front of him, three conservative, pro-Congress intellectuals.

He began to revile Gandhi, the Father of the Nation, the bald anorexic with the grandmother's smile.

'That man!' he said. 'That man in his obscene loincloth, his ribs sticking out!'

He began to deify Subhas Bose, the brilliant, sidetracked Bengali. He radiated with irritable energy, argumentativeness, obstinacy, a remarkable unwillingness to give in. He spoke with true pride of Subhas Bose, pride shone in his eyes, the pride a son feels when he remembers a calumniated father. The boys, following him as he lectured excitedly and paced from room to room, forgot to finish their game, which remained at a promising, preliminary stage; the British would live to fight another day.

In the afternoon, it stopped raining. It was cloudy, humid and hot. Chhordimoni, Sandeep's great-aunt, who had come early that morning, and had stayed back, had spent the morning making little pyramids out of betel-leaves, stuffing them with betel-nuts (the betel-nuts were round as planets and hard as rocks; she broke them into halves and quarters with a sharp and dangerous implement), smearing them with choona. She chewed on one for

hours, her jaws moving imperceptibly. It was a strong and hardy jaw; it was never exhausted. In the afternoon, everyone slept, and nothing moved in the world but Chhordimoni's jaws, with a stubborn, grinding motion that defied logic, with a subtle rhythm, taking utmost pleasure in the betel-leaf.

Chhotomama was asleep, with a half-open book by his side. Sandeep glanced through its pages; it was a novel by Sarat Chandra Chatterjee. Chhotomama's shelves were full of these books: Sarat Chandra, Bibhuti Bhushan, Tarashankar, Rabindranath; like the names of wines, the names of these authors; an entire generation had been drunk with these names.

Sandeep could hardly read Bengali. He could hardly write it. Brought up in Bombay, away from his own province, Bengal, he was one of the innumerable language-orphans of modern India. He was as illiterate in his language as . . . as Chhaya and Saraswati. But he liked opening these classics and looking at the letters while, outside, new rain-bearing clouds moved in the sky. He saw the letters as characters, 'characters' in both senses of the word: ৰ was a fat man standing straight with his belly sticking out, ৯was the fat man scratching his back, ৰ was an adolescent, lately grown tall and awkward, his head bent forward shyly, ১ was a dancer,

his right leg forever lifted in a self-consciously statuesque pose. The letters were intimate, quirky, ancient, graceful, comic, just as he imagined the people of Bengal to be.

It was a time of many insects. The skies were prolific with tiny, beating creatures. In the evening, there would be a tribe of insects of arbitrary sizes and origins by the fluorescent lamp on the wall. This made the lizard happy. When it saw an insect minding its own business by a corner of the wall, its body ticked urgently and accurately, like the hand of a clock that never runs faster or slower than the exact time. It would turn and stop and advance with staccato, Morse-code-like movements—dot-dot-dash-dot-dot—glide forward in a way that was both jerky and streamlined, and seize and swallow the little insect if it was lucky: if the lizard was lucky, that is. One could never manage to see that precise instant, that half-instant, when it actually grasped the insect with its mouth and swallowed it. Now the insect was here, part of the world of creation, and now it was gone, into the underworld of the lizard's belly.

Once, an insect wandered into Babla's ear. Babla, who had dozed off at seven o'clock in the evening, woke with a start and began to cry loudly. The cry turned into the high-pitched wail of the tragedian trying his best

to move his audience. Upon anxious interrogation, he refused to answer, but cried and pointed to his left ear, but not too noticeably, as if he were afraid the insect might take offence and enter his brain.

'It makes a noise,' he wept. 'It crackles.'

Mamima made him lie down. Wave after wave of tears followed; something sad and irreversible seemed to have happened in the house, and only Babla, the youngest child, gave it a voice and expression. Saraswati heated a bowl of oil, Mamima dipped her little finger in it, and holding it an inch away from the earhole, let a drop of oil fall into the dark tunnel. Then another, and another.

'Close your eyes,' she said. 'Don't be a little coward. The insect is more afraid than you are.'

Babla was not convinced. He could not bear the thought of a living creature wandering inside another living creature, himself. He lived alone inside his body; he did not want to share it with an insect. A short while later, a flying-ant came out from the darkness of the tunnel into the dazzling, lighted space of the room. Its wings were sticky with oil, and it stumbled onto the pillow. It seemed overwhelmed by what it had seen in Babla's ear. Mamima killed it swiftly with a magazine, and it appeared quite ready to die, as if its mission in life were now complete.

# 10

Sometime during the rains, Abhi's and Babla's school started again. The last week of Sandeep's summer holidays was spent alone in the daytime, with the house and its uninhabited spaces all to himself. Of course, his mother and his aunt were present, but they were more like the furniture in the house that would always be there and which comforted by their presence—they were more like beds to lie in or chairs to sit safely in rather than companions to conspire with; they would always be there.

With the coming of the rains, Saraswati caught a cold, and her coughs got worse and worse. Without Abhi and Babla around, Sandeep began to see Saraswati as an individual rather than a mythical figure, which was a mildly disturbing experience. When she got fever, she

went up to the terrace and lay upon a mattress beneath the sun. When it rained, she came in. 'Hai hai! O misery!' she exclaimed. She wanted to work, but Mamima had commanded her to rest. 'O misery, misery!' she said. Why did she want to work? Shivering at the same time? It was not because she was good or wonderful (imagine Saraswati being good or wonderful), but because she was frightened of not being needed. Sandeep pitied her, and it hurt him to feel an emotion as elevated as pity for such a crumpled, ugly woman, who could not even talk proper Bengali, who only spoke in a crude village dialect which was a huge source of amusement to the children, and who ate puffed rice soaked in water in the afternoon. Once, when asked to write her name, her fingers, shy and tortured, had scrawled something painful on a piece of paper. There was a fixed smile on Saraswati's face as, far away, her fingers took several minutes to accomplish their task. 'What is this?' they asked mockingly, pointing to the stillborn, deformed word on the paper. 'Who knows?' she replied 'I could never write. Besides, an old woman can't write.' 'How old are you, Saraswati?' they asked her. 'Forty or fifty,' she said. 'I'm not sure.' Forty years for her was a long time, as was fifty years; they were both nearly an eternity but a little less than a lifetime, and she liked both numbers equally. The sense

of time had by-passed her, like a gentle breeze, without disturbing her. What an arrogant woman! Pratap, who got the lowest marks in class, was less ignorant. And now that she was ill, Sandeep pitied her, albeit with difficulty, for he usually reserved emotions like pity for beautiful orphan girls in stories or films. 'Hai hai!' she said. She would not take medicines. Stubborn, pigheaded, stupid woman. Instead, she ate the bitter tulsi leaves of the tulsi plants that grew in pots on the terrace. Bitter, bitter leaves. She too was like the furniture in the house; many, many people had rested in her without knowing it. Old, decaying piece of furniture, never to be removed, giving rest again and again.

At four o'clock each day, the magic moment, Abhi and Babla came back home from school. Sandeep watched them silently from the upper window, his face pressed against the mullions, his hands clutching the long, cold mullions. He felt a light twinge of envy as he watched the porter help them off the schoolbus. When they glanced up and saw him, they waved, and he waved back. This was his way of welcoming them back to the shadowy world of the holidays.

But when they came up, they were full of what they had done at school, what this or that teacher had said, what mischief a friend had been up to. They flung their

bags onto the bed. The bags, made of khaki cloth, were stuffed with textbooks and ragged exercise books that had names and classes written neatly on their brown-paper covers. In some of Abhi's books, Sandeep found the following written on the first page:

Abhijit Das,
17 Vivekananda Road, Calcutta (South),
West Bengal,
India,
Asia,
Earth,
The Solar System,
The Universe.

It was a strange and sublime address.

Now, ripping the shoes off their feet, they roared to Saraswati for food, and began talking about the school play. Sandeep told them in hushed tones, as if he knew what he was about to say was inconceivable:

'Saraswati's not well.'

'Ooof!' said Abhi. 'Why did she have to fall ill *now*?'

Their faces glowed with sweat and the radiance of another excitement. It gave Sandeep a sense of the other world to which they belonged and in which he played

no part; it made his afternoon games with them seem small and temporary. He felt the shadowy, secret life of the holidays, the vivid underground existence during those long afternoons in the house while their parents slept calmly, slip out of his grasp. Yet the three of them, Abhi, Babla and Sandeep, sprawled on the great bed together, and talked and talked, reliving the illusion of togetherness. By simply talking, by simply never ceasing these long, meaningless conversations, Sandeep felt he could buy time and keep the holidays from ending.

It rained during the day, and the old, mysterious sound of thunder rang in the sky. With Abhi and Babla at school, Sandeep lounged in the upper room, lying on his stomach upon the bed, haltingly reading Bengali sentences in a children's magazine, cautiously looking at the pictures. He sometimes found, to his surprise, that it took him a minute to read a single short line of Bengali. He would stare at a difficult word uncomprehendingly for what seemed like hours. How slowly time passed in the last, empty moments of the holidays! The thunder echoed in the sky again, and he was impatient for Abhi to return, so that he could discuss the sound of the thunder with him. He peered at the magazine, and found that it gave him a strange comfort to read these Bengali riddles, limericks, jokes; to hear, through the riddles,

limericks and jokes, the language speaking to him. A fly settled near his hand. Looking up, he saw the lizard motionless upon the wall. By accident, he saw himself in the mirror, lying on the bed, his body relaxed and his face serious. He heard his aunt blowing the conch and ringing the bell in the prayer-room. He wished he could live in the mirror, always, the way he saw himself now, a lazy, motionless image, with the fly and the lizard, the sound of the conch and the rain, the jokes and rhymes in his mother-tongue upon his lips.

In these last days, he grew used to the company of women. He eavesdropped on their conversations; he asked them questions to which only a woman would know the answer. He wandered at large among these slow, motherly figures, these timeless busybodies and humorous samaritans, who went around the world in their long, flowing saris like priests in their robes. To be in this old house in the daytime with his aunt, his mother, Chhordimoni and Saraswati was to see women assume life with an unimpedable vegetable dignity.

When Chhordimoni spent a few days with them, it was a great pleasure for Sandeep to watch her briskly and fiercely ordering the rest of the world about, for she was convinced of its insignificance, as she got a special

meal prepared for the evening. 'Duffer!' she would say to his aunt. 'Is that the way to peel a banana-flower? Give it to me!' She would proceed with trembling hands to peel it, and fail, because she was so old, and unsure of her own movements, though her intellect was clear and frustrated with the aging body it lived in. Often, Sandeep's mother had told him what Chhordimoni was like in her younger days, a portrait of a majestic and imperious woman, whom servants and children were afraid of, grudgingly taken by men as an equal, one of the first women graduates. And now this. 'Here! Take it! Do you think I have time for these things?' she would say, roughly pushing the vegetable back. She would call the washerwoman a fool for putting too much starch in her sari; she would call the vegetable-seller an ass for bringing such sickly-looking aubergines; she would call Saraswati an imbecile for refusing to take medicine. The air rang out with expletives, intense names as untranslatable as poetry: 'Duffer! Crow-face! Retarded child! She-goat! Cow-eyed imbecile!' Sometimes, in a fit of calculated irony and sarcasm, she produced the opposite range of words: 'O genius! O wonder-worker! O helpless child!' When she fell silent, the inspiration seemed to go out of the air, and a great calm settled upon everything.

In one of these serene and silent moments in the afternoon, Sandeep asked her:

'Chhordimoni, how old were you when you got married?'

She was lying on the bed, scarcely listening. From the well of her subconscious, a voice replied:

'I was twenty.'

'Was that a long time ago, Chhordimoni?'

'Yes. Fifty years.' She counted silently to herself. 'Fifty-two years ago.'

'That's a long time,' said Sandeep.

'Yes.'

He paused to think. Then he asked:

'Did you see the Romans, Chhordimoni?'

'No.'

'Did people say "thee" and "thou", Chhordimoni? Did you ever hear them say that?'

'I don't think I did, Mona.'

There was a brief, thoughtful silence. Then:

'When did Chhordamoni die, Chhordimoni?'

'When I was twenty-five, I think.'

'Why did he die, Chhordimoni?'

'He was not well, Mona.'

'Not well like Saraswati?'

'More not-well than Saraswati, Mona.'

Sandeep paused. He could not picture his not-well grand-uncle.

'Did Chhordamoni have a moustache, Chhordimoni?'

'He had a big moustache.'

'Did you have Rabimama and Jatinmama after Chhordamoni died or before he died, Chhordimoni?'

His great-aunt stared thoughtfully at him for a moment. 'Before he died, Mona.'

'Did he play with Rabimama and Jatinmama?'

'There was not much time, Mona. But he did play with them, and he took them out on the horse-carriage . . . though he had a bad temper, sometimes.'

'As bad as yours, Chhordimoni?'

She stared at him with tragic, bewildered eyes. 'I don't have a bad temper, Mona.'

'But sometimes you do, Chhordimoni. Not always, but just sometimes-sometimes.'

'It's only when people are stupid. Now go and bother your aunt and let me sleep.'

She turned over on her side, cracked all her knuckles meticulously, and began to snore almost instantaneously. After regarding the wrinkles on her face and hands for a while, Sandeep crawled over her body to the other side of the bed, where his aunt lay reading the health page of a magazine. He loved crawling like a clumsy,

four-legged beast across and over the bodies of the grown-ups, these warm figures in cool saris, and then curl up between them like a mountain-cat among huge, sheltering boulders.

He nudged his aunt, who lifted an arm and placed it on her forehead, making her bangles sing as she did so.

'Mamima,' he asked, 'when were you married?'

'Why are you interested in our marriages today?' she said without turning her head.

'No, tell me, Mamima, tell me when you got married.'

'I've forgotten.'

'You've not forgotten, Mamima! How can you forget?'

'I tell you I've forgotten.'

'All right, then tell me *where* you got married.'

'I was married here in Calcutta. Your Chhotomama came in a car. He was wearing a white dhuti and a silk panjabi with gold buttons, and a topor on his head. I, of course, didn't see him till later. But my cousin, Beena, saw them coming and she rushed into our room and told me. She said: The bridegroom's come.'

'What did you say?'

'I couldn't say anything, because they were putting chandan and sindoor on my face, and kaajal around my eyes. I wasn't allowed to move.'

'Not even talk?'

'Well, I could talk, but since they were drawing such beautiful patterns on my forehead, I didn't want to spoil it by talking about the bridegroom. Who wants to know about the bridegoom?'

'Weren't you interested?'

'Not in the bridegroom.'

'Had you ever seen him before?' In Sandeep's mind, it was no longer Chhotomama, but some other man who was about to get married to Mamima, who was no longer Mamima, but some other woman.

'Only in a photograph.'

'Did you like him?'

'Not a bit. He had much too big a nose for me. Also, Shampa, my little cousin, who was the only one from our family who had come with them in the car—she was a small, lively girl then, and she wore a blue frock that day—told me that he had argued with the driver all the way about which was the shorter route to Boubazaar.'

'Why did you marry him, then, Mamima?'

'Oh, I liked your mother and Chhordimoni. When I met them, I thought, They're nice people. So, because I wanted to know your mother and Chhordimoni better, I married him.'

'Do you like him now?'

She wrinkled her nose: 'Not at all. He's such a busybody.'

'Why didn't you . . .' he paused emphatically.

'Why didn't I what?'

'Why didn't you have a love-marriage?'

She wrinkled her nose a little more.

'Of course not. How boring!' She was silent, and then said, 'Not knowing the person makes it so much more exciting! It's such a great adventure . . .'

In the course of the conversation, it was divulged that, on the first night, he had asked whether she liked cricket, to which she had replied, No. They had both agreed that they loved Tagore songs and Sachin Deb Burman's voice. He had asked her if she could sing, and she had said no again. So it was he who had sung a song for her, which she had found very funny because of the seriousness of his face, though she had to admit that he sang very well. First she had Abhi, the dark one with large eyes, and they named him Abhijit, another name for Vega, the bright star, and called him Abhi for short. Then they had Babla, the fair one, who looked more like his father, and they named him Surajit, which means the One Who Has Mastered Music, partly because it rhymed with Abhijit, and partly because Chhotomama wanted a son who

could sing. Abhijit and Surajit, two brothers, rhyming names, always arguing with each other. Oh, I remember when Babla was born, said Sandeep. I remember going in the car, which was not so old and run-down then, with Saraswati and Abhi and Ma. I remember the nurses and the doctors with masks on their faces. Do you? asked Mamima, surprised. Yes, I often remember that scene, though I didn't know it was Babla's birth until now. Saraswati loved the child, said Mamima, and then she said conspiratorially, she even nursed him to keep him quiet. Sandeep thought of Saraswati's small, wrinkled breasts. They talked until his aunt was tired and wanted to sleep.

'But what shall I do, Mamima?' Sandeep asked.

'Well, go to the terrace,' she said in a sleep-heavy voice. 'I planted some chilli plants in a pot. See if the chillies are growing, and guard them from bulbuls and parrots.'

So he went upstairs to the terrace to watch the chillies growing.

Saraswati was sleeping on the terrace, a small, huddled figure. The sun was high and scorching, and it was uncomfortably hot, as it always is between rains. Next to her there was a potted tulsi plant, and next to that, two

chilli plants. The chilli blossoms were like little lavender stars; the chillies grew from their centre, fierce pointed clots of purple, each a tiny phallus. Sandeep shooed away two crows that were hopping around the plants with a sly and tactful curiosity; they flew to the terrace of the neighbouring house, and from there to the next house, and then to the next. At each house, they paused like burglars and darted around guiltily, as if they were perpetually on the verge of breaking some law, perpetual trespassers in God's world. Then, quite suddenly, in a fit of candour, they hoarsely declared 'Ka! Ka!' in the reverie of the afternoon. No one woke.

Between two and four o'clock, a golden stupor descended upon the city. Sandeep loved these two hours when it was too hot to move, when the eddying waves of people disappeared and a low tide came upon everything, leaving lane after lane like gullies in the sand and house after house like sandcastles upon an empty beach, when the splendid arguments in the tea-shops came to a brief conclusion, and everyone agreed with everyone and fell silent.

Clothes hung from clotheslines in the terrace, and undulated like many-coloured waves, all at once, when a breeze blew from the direction of the railway lines. They were happy, cheerful flags that signified life in a house.

There were trousers, shirts, petticoats, blouses, and magnificent lengths of saris, each with a different and striking motif, each a small waterfall of life and colour, unravelled to dry. Sandeep had often seen Saraswati unfolding these sinuous boa-constrictors of cloth (how wrinkled they looked, then, bad-tempered and wrinkled, and how rejuvenated they would look tomorrow, when they were ironed and given their customary face-lift), beating them against the air with a single electric movement to rid them of the last drops of water, then clipping them, her arms wide-apart, as if outstretched in a deep and satisfying yawn.

A mist of drowsiness hung over the lanes. In the still houses, families had eaten their lunch of rice, dal and fish and fallen asleep. Afternoon was a time of digestion, a time of fullness and contentment, full bellies and closed eyes. In all the shadowy houses of Calcutta at this moment, the gastric juices were solemnly at work. There was not a movement in the corridors, no noise; yet if you put an ear against the belly of one of these sleepers, you would probably hear a rich gurgling sound.

Not everyone was asleep. People who had had a meal less substantial dotted the lane perfunctorily. Sometimes, a girl came to a terrace, ostensibly to hang, let us say,

a sari on a clothesline; at the same time, a young man appeared on the terrace three houses away, apparently to inspect a water-tank. They glanced at each other, then fumbled with their work, then glanced at each other, then fumbled, then glanced—such shy, piercing glances exchanged in the heat of the afternoon! How straight and undeflected the man's glance travelled, how swift and disguised the woman's answering glance! What rhythm the moment possessed!

Near a derelict tea-shop, a rickshawalla lay slouched in the shade of his rickshaw. Idly, he clapped his hands in the air. After a moment, Sandeep realized he was killing mosquitoes. Clap . . . clap . . . clap . . . clap . . . Four mosquitoes. Clap . . . clap . . . Two more mosquitoes. One was reminded of the joke in which a man whose neck was aching stopped for a minute on the street and turned his head up to ease the pain. People who had been walking past noticed him, and thought that he was watching something terribly interesting and important in the sky. One by one, they stopped beside him and stared up with deep attention. Meanwhile, the first man, feeling somewhat better, continued his journey, leaving everyone else still gazing thoughtfully at the sky. This is what must have happened to Calcutta in the afternoon; the first man had casually walked away; the rest of

Calcutta was still staring at that fascinating, non-existent point in the emptiness, waiting for the revelation.

He heard car-horns blowing in the distance. He heard shouts—a taxi-driver must be insulting a bus-driver. It was the first traffic-jam of the evening, punctual, ceremonial and glorious. The two hours of golden stillness had ended. The cars and crowded buses were on the roads again; Abhi and Babla would come back home from school; pigeons flapped their wings and rose above rooftops, a clean universe of rooftops and terraces. Tomorrow, Sandeep remembered, he would return with his mother to Bombay. He saw Chhaya at the turning of the lane, walking in the direction of the house. It was time—it must be—to sweep the dust from the floors.

# 11

A year and a half passed before Sandeep came to Calcutta again. In Bombay, his father had been promoted to an even higher position in his company. They had moved from their big apartment to an even bigger one; from the twenty-third storey, they had moved to the twenty-fifth storey of a twenty-five storey building. Standing in one of the balconies or looking out from the windows in the hall, one could see almost all of Bombay, the swarms of lights in the evening, the hoods of tiny cars shining and vanishing in the sunlight during the daytime—a view marginally more breathtaking and marginally more unreal than the one seen from the balcony of the twenty-third floor. No sounds, no smells, only a pure, perpetually moving picture.

One and a half years after the last holidays, Sandeep

and his parents visited Calcutta in the winter. Sandeep felt what a statue in a museum would feel if he suddenly came to life and walked out into a shimmering crowd of people. Because it was a little cold now in Calcutta, people swathed themselves in shawls, mufflers, sweaters, coats and several kinds of woollen garments. The first thing one saw when one came to Calcutta in December was a welter of warm clothes. As usual, the people of Calcutta did everything to excess; the streets had the air of a fancy-dress party as shawls and cardigans and jackets floated by solemnly. In the nights, when it became really cold, beggars set fire to old rubber tyres, and sat around the circles of slow flame to warm their hands.

The presence of Sandeep's father gave the holidays a mood of optimism and potential. They listed the things they would do and the families they would visit together. Endless questions were asked by Sandeep to which his father provided endless answers. Besides, his father would have a car at his service which they would use when he was not attending business lunches. This would be useful as Chhotomama had had to sell his car; Sandeep remembered the old, battered Ambassador and wondered where it was now; to whom did it belong? Sandeep remembered the dials on its dashboard which

always showed that the fuel-tank was empty and that the car was running at twenty kilometres per hour, and he remembered the torn leather upholstery and the shuddering doors.

His father's presence also meant that this time they would be staying at the Grand Hotel on Chowringhee. The company was going to meet all the expenses, naturally. The thrill of exploring the large lobby with its mirrors and sofas, of dining at the restaurant at night while a band played and couples danced, of gazing out at the swimming-pool in the afternoon, of following the uniformed bearers with their trays, soon died out. At such times, Sandeep deserted his parents shamelessly and spent days and nights at the old house with his cousins.

Not much had changed in the old house. But the few changes that had taken place had had their effect. For one thing, the car had been sold—this meant that Chhotomama had to wake up earlier in the mornings, make a great deal more noise, bother everyone a great deal more, and rush out to catch his bus or train with more than his usual fanfare. Around him, Mamima and Saraswati performed their old desperate dance, which was a little more desperate now, and a little less like a dance. When he returned in the evenings, he

looked soiled and tired from standing in the bus and in numberless, undisciplined queues; so he had a second bath in the evening, and his songs echoed once more in the bathroom:

*Godhulir chhaya pathe*
*Je gelo chini go tare.*

Whenever he sang those songs, the tunes cleansed the atmosphere as the trickle of water from the shower cleansed the soil and smears of dirt from his body.

The other change that had taken place in the one and a half years was to do with Abhi. He had been transferred from a Bengali-medium school to a famous English-medium one. This would increase his prospects at the age of twenty-one, when he would graduate from college and start looking for a job. He would be what the world wanted him to be—smart, English-speaking and brittle, like one of those ideal men in cigarette advertisements. But his prospects now, at the age of ten, did not look very bright. He was having trouble with this strange new language, English. Sometimes, when he wrote his answers in class, his teachers pointed out that they did not make sense. He would have liked to point out to them that it was the language that did not make sense.

It was a riddle; it was difficult and unapproachable. At home, he had taken to sitting at his study-table with an English grammar in front of him, his eyes gazing dreamily out of the window at the palm tree in the backyard and the terrace of the professor's house. He could gaze at the palm tree and the professor's house for hours. This habit had earned him a nickname from his friends—The Poet. Abhi, the poet . . .

In the winter, the days ended early. Smoke rose from earthen ovens and wood fires into the air, and hung mysteriously over the lanes in the evenings. Abhi's new tutor came on these smoky evenings, every Monday, Wednesday and Friday, tinkling his bicycle after the sun had gone down. Abhi, Babla and Sandeep would peer from the balcony as he came in, and groan inwardly. They would recognize him at once because of the red muffler wrapped so carefully around his head—nothing was visible of his face but his spectacles. From upstairs, he looked somewhat like a burglar, a rather harmless, officious-looking burglar. He would unwrap the muffler, folding it into neat little folds; Abhi would watch in fascination, hoping the folds would be folded into tinier folds, hoping he would never finish folding his muffler. Then he would climb up the stairs calling—Aabhi. Aaabhi. Aaaabhi—the first syllable getting longer and

grander all the time. Abhi would wait till the first syllable had become ominously and inordinately long, and then he would go dutifully to the stairs to greet him. If there was a power-cut, he would stand at the head of the stairs with a lantern in his hands watching his tutor grope his way up, clutching the bannisters, as large shadows flickered and trembled on the wall.

While Abhi worked with his tutor, Sandeep and Babla spied on them from the corridor and made rude comments about the size of the tutor's ears. Sometimes, Abhi would take a break to drink water or to go to the toilet, at which the boys would be reunited briefly to gossip busily about the tutor and break into fits of silent giggles. They were not sure what it was exactly that they were laughing about, but this did not stop them from finding the situation impossibly funny. After a minute, the tutor would say, 'Abhi, come back to your books now,' at which Abhi's eyes would become sad and pensive, the eyes of a man with many responsibilities.

When the English lessons began, the voice became stentorian and English sentences and words exploded like little bombs in the air.

—Whut ees thee name of thee boy?
—Thee name of thee boy ees John.

—Whut deed John habhfor deenar?

—John had meelk and bredfor deenar.

—*Why* deed John habh meelk and bredfor deenar?

The question was not to be answered, because Saraswati came in with a cup of tea and a plate of dark sweetmeats. 'Aaah!' said the tutor, lapsing back into his mother-tongue. 'Lovely tea!' It was a pleasure to hear his natural eloquence in Bengali after his brave guerrilla invasion into the rocky terrain of English; silence descended as he drank his tea, no noise but that of passionate, noisy sips, and there was a temporary respite from the savage bombardment of those foreign words on this helpless, sleepy room. There was a lull, and an 'all-clear' atmosphere prevailed.

Chhotomama's business was faring worse than ever. Yet who would have suspected it? Certainly the children suspected nothing. They lived in their own world which was half illusion, because it was founded so much on fantasy, and half real, palpably real, because its tissue was wholly made of sensations. When they would grow up, and their lives and the lives of the grown-ups would be retold, they would seem like fairy-tales and legends. Certainly, they suspected nothing. They

roamed in a silent, self-created web of sounds, smells and colours. Once, Sandeep had woken late in the night to find Chhotomama standing at the window near the bed smoking a cigarette. The moonlight dimmed outlines and made tangible things seem intangible, and Chhotomama and the furniture in the room appeared like figures on the wrong side of a tapestry; everything seemed to be dissolving into the smoke Chhotomama was exhaling from his nostrils. Hearing Sandeep stir, Chhotomama had turned to him and said: 'Aren't you asleep, Mona? There, go to sleep now, it's very late. Go to sleep.' There was affection and assurance in the voice, and affection in the touch of the hand as it stroked his hair.

In the winter, Calcutta was at its most beautiful. At eleven o'clock in the morning, when it was not too chilly, Saraswati brought pails of steaming hot water, which she had heated downstairs, slowly and laboriously up to the bathroom. The children were stripped naked and bathed; they gasped in pleasure and terror as someone dipped a mug in the bucket and poured great, eloquent splashes of hot water on their heads. Later, shivering and still naked, they would troop into the room and stand in a patch of warm winter sunlight in front of the window. A mother

or an aunt would hold their faces firmly, imprinting, upon their defenceless cheeks, the furious marks of her fingers, and one by one, comb their moist black hair with murderous pleasure. A crow would caw in alarm.

'Ma . . . ma . . . my parting is slightly more on the side.'

'Hold still!'

A servant-woman would be staring from the terrace of the next house at the brown, gleaming buttocks of the children. When the little show was over, she would reluctantly tie the aanchal of her sari tightly around herself and resume her work. The crow, who had also been watching with interest, would fly away from the window in pursuit of more pressing matters. There would be a smell of talcum powder and Jabakusum oil in the air.

In the evenings, Chhotomama would come home and have a small simple meal of yoghurt and khoi and slices of bananas, mixed together with sugar, the smallest, simplest meal a Bengali can have. As he sat in the verandah and ate this from a bowl with a spoon, the taste of it reminded him of his childhood, for he had first had this mixture from his mother's fingers as a child. Each time he put a small dollop of the yoghurt in his mouth, and chewed on the khoi patiently he tasted his childhood. It was made of the sourness of yoghurt,

the sweetness of sugar, and the grey taste of bananas. Also the warmth of his mother's fingers from which he ate the mixture. It was as if his memory resided in the small, invisible taste-buds in his tongue rather than in his brain. Around him, voices rose and scattered in the lane.

Later, he went to the bathroom and began singing. Sandeep's mother and father would come from the Grand Hotel in the car; Shonamama and Chhordimoni would arrive on a rickshaw, and if it was Abhi's unlucky day, his tutor would follow closely on a bicycle. There would be a sound of footsteps and laughter in the house, and the smell of sandalwood incense. Smoke hung over the lane, delicately bandaging the decaying walls of the houses. At the turning of the lane, boys played badminton in a small, square lawn in the glare of electric lights. The world happened in slow motion; the shuttlecock rose and fell in slow motion.

When Sandeep and his cousins ran up to the terrace to spy on the world, they saw the moon and the great constellations in the sky. It was a clear sky, and the clouds seemed to have descended upon Calcutta; rivers of smoke and mist travelled through the streets, blurring the lights in the houses. House after house stood like a little island surrounded by smoke. This is what it must

be like, Sandeep thought, to live inside a crater, the fumes putting you to sleep, each day the last day before the eruption. When he went downstairs, and heard the grown-ups laughing and drinking tea, Saraswati closing windows to prevent mosquitoes from coming in and smoke from filling the room, and Chhotomama singing in the bathroom accompanied by great splashes of water, he wanted to tell them to tell stories all night long, because the day of the eruption had come, finally. But when Saraswati shut all the windows, he felt the brightly lit room was safe, and that the house, like a patient, enduring ark built by the hands of an infinitely wise man, would carry them away over the tide. In the bathroom, Chhotomama was singing:

Whether you'll remember me or not, I have
   forgotten.
(splash of water) . . .
Moment after tiny moment, I come to your door,
   sing without cause.
Days pass; I remain; if ever, on the road, I find
   myself near you,
(two splashes of water) . . .
I long to see a smile of startled peace upon your face.
That is why I sing without cause.

Another loud splash of water, then the sound of water draining away, then silence, as he dried himself, then again:

> Spring-flowers drift to the earth; springtime comes
>     to a close.
> It has filled an instant's fist; it need know nothing
>     more.
> The day will end, the light draw to a fineness,
>     the song cease, the instrument be silent.
> As long as I'm here, won't you load with riches this
>     mock-raft of mine?
> That is why I sing without cause.

The sound of Saraswati shutting the windows in the other room, the footsteps of his aunt coming up the stairs with two cups of tea in her hands, and the sound of the grown-ups talking, falling silent, talking, falling silent, like the advance and retreat of a tide.

# 12

The next day, Chhotomama had a heart attack. (The doctors later clarified that it wasn't an attack, but a spasm. The heart's dance has its own rules and nuances.) At around eleven-thirty in the morning, when the children had come out of the bath, and Mamima was in the prayer-room, blowing the conch and arranging the offering of fruit and batashas for the gods, Chhotomama, who was planning to take a late bus to work, was standing by the basin, rubbing his chest and making funny noises with his throat.

'It's wind,' he was saying. 'What *have* they given me for breakfast?'

Everything was quite beautiful at that moment, and Saraswati was combing the children's hair. The maidservant in the neighbouring house was pottering

about as usual on the neighbouring terrace. Flies were dancing gracefully in front of the mirror, and the sun kept coming out of and going back behind clouds, so that there were phases of light and shade in the world, as if a giant bird were flying across the sun, and obstructing, partially, the sunlight with its slow moving wings. Sandeep's mother was going to come from the Grand Hotel in the car; the driver would blow the horn announcing her arrival; she would take them out to lunch. Possibly, Chhotomama would take a lift from them, and Sandeep imagined the car crammed with human beings, talking busily about trivial and exciting things.

But all the plans would have to be changed now, because Chhotomama was having a heart attack. All the plans would have to be different now. Quite unexpectedly, there he was, rolling on the bed, making an odd grunting sound, desperately trying to tear his shirt off. The buttons were coming apart, exploding like peas and falling to the floor. He was jumping up, falling back, rolling from side to side, like an acrobat doing a bizarre act to impress the children. Any moment, perhaps, he would rise and touch the ceiling. The children were staring with open mouths, and Saraswati, smiling like an infant watching a tiger at the zoo, was

still combing their hair. Her hands were trembling, as if they alone understood the terror of what was happening.

'Dada . . .' she whispered. 'Dada . . .'

He roared now, and the shirt tore in his hands with a long hissing sound. Then he was silent. The comb dropped to the ground, but did not break, and Saraswati rushed forward, her white sari falling around her like a lowered flag. She called out for Mamima. The sound of the conch, the rich, powerful sound, born of human breath, that had such conviction it seemed the walls of the house would collapse, and the ringing of the bell, the heart of music at the centre of prayer, stopped abruptly. In the distance, there was a sound of a plate being upset or overturned, and the soft, hurrying patter of bare feet. At an even greater distance, on the horizon of hearing, a car blew its horn again and again in the lane.

Chhotomama did not want to go to hospital. 'It's wind,' he was insisting, while Mamima and Sandeep's mother shook their heads. The children floated like satellites in the distance, afraid to collide with the painful orbit of adult lives, and yet always being pulled toward it against their will. Saraswati took the company car to fetch the doctor, because the telephones were not working in the area. There was a power-cut, and Sandeep's mother

began to fan her brother with a newspaper. 'It's all right,' he said. 'Nothing's happened.' He started to criticize the government for its inability to rectify the power shortage. Then he vomited, and the vomit was a small yellow puddle on the floor. 'That,' he said, pointing to the puddle, 'that's what has been doing it.' He was triumphant. 'Today's breakfast.' The doctor came with many instruments, siphons and tubes. 'Breathe,' he said. He was pressing a kind of pump and doing all kinds of things at once. 'The ECG,' he said. His assistant, an adolescent boy, took out a bundle of filaments which the doctor attached to Chhotomama's body. There they looked like coiled nerves that had mistakenly tapered out of Chhotomama's skin, or thin tuberous plants that had started growing from his hands and feet. Next to him a square machine hummed now and then in a bored manner. An interesting, indecipherable graph was drawn on a strip of paper which the machine stuck out like an endless tongue. Everything somehow depended on the mysterious code written on this strip of paper, which the doctor was now looking at. 'The hospital,' he said, when he had finished. Suddenly, the power came back, and the fan began to turn, making a peaceful, whirring sound, throwing a breeze on all their faces. When they tried to get Chhotomama into the car, they found he could

not stand up. The doctor and the company driver had to help him, one of Chhotomama's arms around each neck. Mamima was crying in a strange way, pressing the loose end of her sari upon her face, covering her mouth and nose with it like a muffler, as if she were feeling cold. Chhotomama was laughing and saying, 'Don't be silly.' The children were standing there, watching the faces, the clothes, the lips, the eyes, the movements that were now hurried and now calm, the tears, surprisingly adult tears, salty with unknown experience, the exact way in which they streamed from the eyes.

On the way to the hospital, Chhotomama had another attack. He vomited on the floor of the company car. The driver, caught in a traffic-jam, shook his head from side to side. He had seen these things happen to his elder brother, who had died in half an hour. His father had died in his village from cholera, which was a different kind of disease. He began to think of his father, and those last moments when nothing could help him.

In hospital, they put Chhotomama on oxygen in the Intensive Care Unit. The relatives arrived in rickshaws, trams, taxis; some walked, some came by bus; some came alone, some in families, some with their friends. Some came with their hair still gleaming after a bath;

some came unshaven with stubble on their cheeks; some came in newly pressed clothes; a few came in clothes they had slept in. Some had asked for the day off at the office; some had come without telling anyone. One by one, or family by family, they walked in and sat in the Waiting Room, ruminating, asking questions, speaking to each other in the dialect of their village. Later, the relatives who lived furthest away from the rest spoke about what they were doing now and what their sons were doing now and which daughter was going to get married to whom. The days were short and in a few hours it became dark, and the lights were turned on in the Waiting Room, where the relatives still sat talking, sipping now and then from a flask, eating dry, crumbling sweetmeats from paper containers, shawls around their shoulders, huddled as if it were a picnic in a hill-station.

Shonamama and Sandeep's father had spent most of the time with the doctors and the heart specialist. Now they came down the stairs gravely.

'How is he?' someone asked. 'Does he have a chance?'

There was something faintly indecent about the second question. Why should anyone know if he had a chance? Dying is not a horse-race. There should be no speculation about the ending, no wagers won or lost. No

one need know anything but basic information provided from moment to moment.

'He's still in danger,' said Sandeep's father.

As if on cue, a woman began to cry in a silly, high-pitched voice.

'Stop it!' Shonamama said. A feeling of anxiety passed like a delicate wave over the crowd of relatives. Mamima and Sandeep's mother comforted each other in whispers. Someone turned on a small transistor radio to listen to the news, and a tiny, crackling voice with a clear accent pronounced the names of different towns and different countries, and large, remote events. The mind was soothed by that great fantasy world of politics and government the radio spoke of. The children, everywhere at once, were playing among themselves, running frantically through the gleaming corridors of the hospital, imitating the busy doctors and peering fugitively at the patients, mingling with the crowds of visitors like spies. They walked to the hospital gates and made friends with the watchman with the big moustache, who was in a khaki uniform and held a long stick in his hand. In his cap and shoes, he was a commander, a glamorous emblem from a storybook. The boys roamed through the wide, well-kept lawns on the hospital grounds, and explored the shrubs and

trees in the garden. With the instant recognition of the aesthete, they realized the hospital had the potential for being an inexhaustible playground, one such as they'd never entered before. They noted the ambulances as they came in, and they played hide-and-seek in the parking-lot, where cars that belonged to visitors and patients' relatives were parked in rows. Car after car after car, patient after patient, anxious family after anxious family, car after car with the windows rolled up, or the driver dozing inside, or the windshield reflecting the last rays of the sun and the images of enormous clouds passing splendidly and oceanically across it as on a screen, car after car, meditative and pensive and silent in the darkening twilight, and the children wandering between them, Sandeep and Abhi crouched in the shadows, and Babla searching for them, calling out their names hesitantly.

Little by little, the relatives trickled out of the hospital and diminished into their own lives. A solitary young man among them was going to spend the night at the hospital, in case of an emergency. He sat there bravely, his shawl wrapped around him tightly, like a sari around a shy woman. Sandeep's father, his mother, Mamima, Chhordimoni and Shonamama got into the car, the

children sitting restlessly on their laps; tonight, they were all going to spend the night in the old house together.

The return was difficult and sombre, as was the adjustment to the ways of life that had become suddenly unreal. Slowly and without interest, they ate their dinner. They drank many glasses of water, however; their thirst seemed unquenchable. Later, they went upstairs, where they would lie on the beds and talk, and in the process, fall asleep, giving up their consciousness in the middle of a word.

But before they slept, Saraswati hung large, rippling mosquito-nets around the beds, because winter was a time of mosquitoes. The room, with its ancient, brown furniture, the clothes hanging from the clothes-horse, the timeless wall-lizard, the clock and the radio on the cupboard, the photographs and portraits of grandfathers and grandmothers, surrounded them, giving them a sense of objects and things that lived always in the present; it was a relief for them that there were so many things in the room that did not possess a past or a future. The room itself was timeless, without beginning or end. The furniture and the wall-lizard symbolized another world, another order of calm, inviolable existence. Outside, rickshawallas sang tunelessly and clapped their hands in the cold, with a small wood fire before them.

Their tuneless song and their clapping hands were also a part of this other existence, this bottomless being. In the city, the winter smoke hung its giant cobwebs between the houses, or stood between each house and the darkness like a lovely, protective mosquito-net. It kept the houses warm and healed the fractures in their walls and kept out the bad dreams of the night and the memories of the day. It too was a part of that other blind existence that happened around the small, painful lives of human beings.

Abhi, Babla, Sandeep and Chhordimoni were going to sleep in the large bed. Because the nights were cold and the dawns chilly, a great soft-textured quilt, which yielded to the fingers like bread, had been provided for them. It had fresco-like patterns on it which seemed to retain a glow even in the dark. They dipped their bodies into its generous warmth, and pulled down the mosquito-net from the four poles that had been screwed on like a ship's rigging to the four corners of the bed. The quilt was like a spacious cave in which their legs roamed and scurried with the exuberance of little bears. Cold outside, and so warm inside—body rubbing against body, like triplets inside the safe obscurity of a womb. Someone turned off the lights, and the mosquito-net shimmered around them like white sails. It had been

an eventful day, but already the children had forgotten its sadness, except in a remote, abstract way. They surrendered themselves to the sensation of the present, to this ship with white sails raising its anchor and drifting toward another harbour.

# 13

Chhotomama did not die. The children had never expected him to, so the fact did not come as any surprise to them. Abhi and Babla knew that their father was ill, but deep down they were convinced he was immortal. So, when their faces became serious, it was less because they were worried on account of their father and more because they enjoyed imitating the serious expressions on the grown-ups' faces. It was a strange and new experience for them, this seriousness.

Of course, it was inconceivable to many of the grown-ups as well that Chhotomama should die. The doctors, at one point, had believed that he was in serious danger. But death was quite inconceivable to the relatives in the Waiting Room. Death was like a miracle; like the camel passing through the needle's eye. How could a flesh-

and-blood human being, who had accumulated such layers of significance in the consciousness of people who knew him, suddenly disappear into nothingness through a point one could not even see? It was a miracle impossible to believe in. It is easier for the imagination to conceive of presences that do not exist—God, angels, demons—than conceive how someone who does exist can cease to be.

A trickle of relatives came in during the day and congregated as usual in the Waiting Room; after sunset, nearly all of them were there, keeping vigil, making themselves useful in some obscure way, or useless in a way that was oddly touching. During visiting hours, people were allowed to go into the Intensive Care Unit, but not more than one at a time, each with a small ticket in his hand. When Sandeep went in through a door at the end of two flights of stairs and a long corridor, he saw Chhotomama lying on a high bed, a sheet and a blanket covering his body. There was a faint, welcoming smile on his face; around him, there were other presences—one could call them nothing else—lying in postures of fatigue or serene relaxation on their beds. The room was cool, and dark and ordered like the inside of an office: it was as if a bizarre board meeting were being held, with directors gathered silently on beds instead of chairs. Sandeep did

not know what to talk to Chhotomama about; he felt too nervous to look directly at him; he was afraid he might see a halo around his head or horns coming out from behind his ears. In fact, it was Chhotomama who had to speak to Sandeep in whispers and put him at his ease, as is so often the case; the sick man having to cheer up his visitor, instead of the other way round. He asked:

'What have you been doing, Mona?'

'Nothing.'

'Have you seen any films lately?'

'No.'

'Have you read any books that are interesting?'

'No.' Then, thoughtfully and shyly, he added, 'There's going to be a Book Fair next week in the maidan. We're going to go there.'

Chhotomama smiled and looked at him from his pillow. It was so beautiful, getting to know his nephews, his sons, his brother, his sister and his wife once again, probing them gently with trivial questions, renewing his acquaintance with them, rediscovering their quirks and oddities which he had known for a lifetime, now, back from death, feeling a delicate surge of pleasure as he recognized these little tics and jerks of movement and speech which constituted a life.

'And what books will you buy?'

'I don't know . . . Mysteries, ghost stories . . . The ones with the best pictures.'

Chhotomama recalled the annual Book Fair which was held around this time of the year in the maidan near St Paul's Cathedral. He remembered the stalls, makeshift temples of books, and the people queueing outside with a religious concentration and devotion. He remembered drifts of people inspecting and sifting through books, opening and shutting hardbound editions, cloth-covered editions, paperback editions. How often he had met old college friends and their children wandering through the crowds. And once the fair was over, that miniature cardboard city would be taken apart, the books would vanish, the crowds disappear, and the maidan would be empty, as if one elaborate mirage had dissolved once you came too near it.

'When is your school opening, Mona?'

'School starts in two weeks,' said Sandeep with an affected weariness. 'But Ma has told me we're going to be here for another month till you get well, so I'll be missing school for two weeks, but Baba will write to the teachers for permission, so it's going to be all right.' He said all this in a great rush, and was pleased and relieved when he had finished.

'Oh I see,' said Chhotomama. 'Well you can start

doing your homework here, when you have nothing else to do.' Sandeep decided it was time to tactfully change the subject. Lifting the small paper box he had been clutching with both hands so far, he said:

'Ma gave you this. There's a sandesh from *Saryanarayan's* inside, and the doctor said you could have it.'

Chhotomama took the box from his hands.

'Oh, sandesh . . . Very nice, very nice.' He opened the box. In the centre was a single white crumbly sweetmeat, made from cottage cheese and dried milk, shaped like a tiny fish with infinitesimal milky-white scales upon it. It had a little milky eye and an open mouth. When Sandeep had gone, Chhotomama ate it in the cool, dark room, and the sweet, crumbling fish disappeared magically from his fingers. Later, he disinterestedly regarded his companions, gathered in this station between one world and another, some with tubes sending a thin stream of oxygen into their nostrils. He looked down again at the paper box, and gazed at the word 'sandesh' printed on its side in neat, stylish Bengali letters:

The letters, curving, undulating, never still, curving into a kinetic life of their own, reminded him of Calcutta, of buying and selling, of people on the pavements, of office-goers in the mornings, and homecomings in the evenings, of children reading books, of arguments and dissensions in the tea-shops, of an unexpected richness in myriad rooms, all festivities of colour and light. He wanted to return to the city where all things curved and arched and danced like those letters; it exhausted him to lie in this room with these other still figures. He longed to come back to life.

A few days later, Chhotomama was moved from the Intensive Care Unit with its sad phantoms into a medium-sized, sunlit room of his own. The doctors were satisfied, the nurses were happy, the relatives were cautious and grateful. Mamima and Sandeep's mother were now permitted to bring him a home-cooked meal of freshwater rohu fish cooked in a tablespoon of oil, with no salt or spices, but with a hint of turmeric and a mild seasoning of black jeera seeds for flavouring and colour. The women seemed to have gained a new buoyancy and purpose in the house; they wandered about in the kitchen with the absorption and abstraction that poets and writers display when they are trying to pin down

a sensation into an exact formula of words without reducing its immediacy. When the faint aroma of the fish preparation drifted through the air, they breathed deeply, in a satisfied way, as if the moment of subtle inspiration had passed, leaving them fulfilled. It was pleasing to see them being themselves; in the past two weeks, they had talked only of expenses and mistakes and hopes, and, most of all, the past and the future; it was pleasing to see them once more apotheosize and transform the present. In the past two weeks, they had not been able to sleep at nights, but had lain awake, fidgeting and stirring, moving from side to side with a short clink and clash of bangles. Night had left them alone with their thoughts behind the mosquito-nets, details about a marriage, funny, unbearable anecdotes about a brother and a sister. But when dawn came, and the first sounds of the city, immemorial sounds, rose in the sky, and the sun shone on the beads of frost, and the newspaper-boy and the men at the underground resumed their work, and Saraswati could be heard tinkering remotely in the kitchen, and the crow cawed at the window, then they felt safe and calm, they slept happily in the first busy and noisy hours of daylight. The noise of the city drowned out the noise in their heads and lulled them to sleep. It had been like that for the past two weeks.

Chhotomama liked his new room in the hospital. He grew increasingly cheerful. He had magazines to read, and even a little transistor radio on which he listened to the news and the sports commentary. In the evening, a stream of visitors came in, and Chhotomama reached new, unspeakable heights of happiness by just looking at the variousness and munificence of the clothes that people wore. After a day of white skirts, white caps, white overcoats, he found himself noticing the details of a sari or the subtle gradations of colour on a shawl, or the differences in dress between one generation and another that he had never taken the trouble to notice before. When his wife came to him, it was her Murshidabad silk sari with the wide red border that caught his eye first, prompting some faculty in his subconscious to throw up a welter of confused images from his childhood, of girls in saris returning home from school in the afternoon, and his mother bending down to water a tulsi plant in the verandah. He seemed to have become a child again, seeing things in startling and disturbing images. If a child could remember and record its first impressions after being born, the initial sense of colours and smells and faces as person after person leaned towards its cot and peered at it, scrutinized it, if it could retell its story of its first day in the world, would it be something like this?

But there were times, in the afternoon, when Chhotomama would wake from a nap and find himself facing a bright, hard wall. At first, it surprised him with its sheer presence. Slowly, he came to realize that it was his future he was looking at. There it was, bright and tangible, with the sunlight falling on it peculiarly. Year after year seemed to have passed since he left his house that winter morning, and he had ended here, facing this wall. He would have to start all over again, he told himself. With his eyebrows screwed gently, he tried to solve the problem the way he had tried to solve his first problem in arithmetic at school. All over again, he told himself, From the beginning . . . Especially for the children. He had married late, he had begun life late. He had responsibilities to his wife, years younger than him, he had responsibilities towards his children. They were, after all, still children.

But, suddenly, the visitors started coming in, and he had no time to think, he was forced to forget. Being ill was a kind of entertainment, a communal ceremony; it involved such a lot of people. He had never seen so many people gathered in one room—three generations, at times—since his wedding or the time when he had passed his BA (Hons) with a first class. Was he being married again, then? Had he got another degree? Was

he dreaming? It was as if they were congratulating him rather than commiserating with him. There was so much laughter. Yet there was grief also. There was comedy. Yet there was seriousness. It was strange how these people managed to hold both in fine balance at the same time.

# 14

Every evening, in the garden, recuperating patients were taken around in wheelchairs by their nurses, or allowed to take gentle walks, with the firm and cautious hand of a nurse on the shoulder. The patients wore loose white shirts and white pyjamas, and each walked slowly and consideringly past the trees, taking one step at a time, like a giant treading carefully between one continent and another, anxious not to trample on an invisible city or a civilization. The children watched them in awe, and with another emotion they had not yet identified, which was pity. Each looked like an Adam who had been expelled from his sacred garden, and now, grown old, had been permitted to reenter, to relearn his old ways and his own, most simple, movements.

At night, after they had said goodbye to Chhotomama, they returned homeward through the lit lanes and alleys of Calcutta. Watching the lanes, they temporarily forgot their own lives, and, temporarily, their minds flowed outward into the images of the city, and became indistinguishable from them. Even at night, the streets were theatres full of actors and extras: reckless dogs, insufferable cows lying in the centre of the lane, families arguing, old women gossiping, children chasing cats, rickshawallas idling, Vaishnav devotees singing religious songs for all to hear. As they watched from the car, they were charmed by the illusion, some nagging uncertainty in their minds was soothed into extinction, they briefly merged with this vague, vast enterprise in which everyone seemed to be taking part.

In some lanes, as they passed, they saw marriages. They saw cars and rickshaws with people getting out of them, people carrying gifts, approaching gates covered with intricate garlands and festoons, and the sound of the shehnai, rich, leisurely, half mournful and half serene, with the special sadness of the human voice, filling the lane with the notes of the Raga Shankara or the Raga Bhairavi. Listening, Sandeep, Abhi and Babla fell asleep, Sandeep's head against Babla's, Babla's head against Abhi's, as if they were dreaming the same dream.

Towards the end of January, the people of Calcutta celebrated the festival of the goddess Saraswati. In every house and lane, offerings were made punctiliously to the austerely beautiful goddess of the arts and of learning. Students would scribble 'Nama Saraswati Nama' a hundred and eight times on a piece of paper so that they might pass their exams. Painters would say a silent prayer for their paintings, and musicians for their music. Writers would ask the goddess to bless the new book they had written: bless this book . . . bless these words. Saraswati, riding a swan, playing the veena with long, attentive fingers, would listen to everyone and promise nothing.

Mamima, too, had brought a small, earthen idol of the goddess. She was going to pray for Chhotomama's health, though this was perhaps somewhat outside the goddess's domain. Yet surely . . . The deity looked so kind and calm and generous. Her mere presence was comforting. There she sat at the end of the room, like a shy bride too diffident to converse with the rest of the family. Surely she would understand Mamima's prayer, this goddess of art and learning.

They decorated the floor before the idol with circular and geometrical motifs, using rice-paste to draw the little and large designs. The women wore new, starched

saris, which swelled unmanageably around them like plumage; the starch made the cotton cloth crispy, gave it the texture of a potato wafer. As they bent to make the patterns on the floor, the white paste oozing from their fingers, now stooping, now rising, the ends of their saris skimming gently behind them like wings, they reminded one of grave birds dancing in a clearing. Gazing at the white loops and spaces that multiplied in constellations on the floor, Sandeep, the ever-curious, asked:

'What's this called?'

'Alpana,' his aunt replied, her voice muffled and faraway in the concentration of the moment. Sandeep remembered a girl he had once known, a girl who could never keep still, called Alpana. Now he knew what the name meant. He did not know what to do with his unexpected knowledge. But he felt a slight, almost negligible, twinge of pleasure, as a meaning took birth in his mind, and died the next instant.

And Abhi, clutching Saraswati's wrinkled hand, always joking at her expense, pointed at the idol and chided:

'Is that you, Saraswati? Is that you?'

'Listen to what he says!' said the old woman, shocked.

Blasphemy and tenderness mingled in the air. Mamima blew the conch, and there was a smell of

sandalwood incense. The offering, made of khoi, milk, bananas and sago seeds, was distributed in small, polished bowls and given to everyone in the house: Shonamama, Chhordimoni, Sandeep and his parents, Abhi and Babla, the sweeper who had dropped in while passing, Saraswati the goddess and Saraswati the maidservant, and Mamima herself. In a bowl kept separate from the rest, she saved a little to take to Chhotomama in the hospital, who did not believe in the gods and goddesses, but loved the rituals and the taste of the offerings.

It was the first week of February when Chhotomama was told he could leave the hospital. The doctor held a small but serious conference in Chhotomama's room, and addressed him in a priestly voice for all to hear: 'Although you are returning home, you must, from the day you return, attempt to change your lifestyle.' Leaning forward in the manner of an elder brother, he confided, though everyone was listening: 'You are too easily excited, too enthusiastic about trivial things. You must try to be more restful, more calm. You will have to lead a more thoughtful—a more disciplined—life from now on. Certain things are out of bounds for you.' He smiled. 'But you will get used to it.' He stopped smiling.

'You will have to get used to it . . . Bed-rest for the first week at home. Spend your time reading, listening to music. By all means, listen to the sports commentary on the radio, but try not to get too excited about the result.' He paused, and smirked cunningly. 'Which team do you support, East Bengal, or Mohun Bagan?' 'Mohun Bagan,' said Chhotomama guiltily. 'Well, from today, you must support *both* teams.' He looked around for approval for this brilliant suggestion. The others smiled vaguely and obsequiously. He continued, 'No rich food. No salt in your diet. No walking up and down the stairs. When you resume your normal life finally, you must, for the first two weeks, climb or descend the stairs one step at a time, taking a ten-second break between each step.' He smiled and slowly repeated, 'One—step—at—a—time—'

In the hospital garden, the sajana tree had broken into white blossoms. In a month, the gulmohur trees would explode into fierce orange flowers, in an undifferentiated, trembling orange mass, with the effect of a volcano erupting and balancing, momentarily, the unspilled lava in its mouth. Small, green, unripe mangoes hung from the mango trees, and bees floated in the air, as if controlled by invisible threads. Between the green lanes of new, nervous leaves, the inmates of the hospital walked as usual in their loose white shirts and

pyjamas. Sandeep looked at them from the bushes. He remembered what Shonamama had once told him about ghosts, how they roamed through the world, touching and observing and smelling it, themselves unsmelt, untouched, unobserved, taking pleasure in the tangible and then melting into their own afterlife.

And somewhere in the trees, the kokil had begun to sing in its clear and piercing voice, till another kokil answered its mating cry, so that a system of musical echoes, of birdcalls mirroring each other, was set up in the garden as the patients walked and the children paused to listen.

Ku-wu

Ku-wu

Ku-wu

There was something questioning and wondering about the cry, but at times it resembled an exclamation, so that it either sounded like Ku-wu? or Ku-wu!, as if a child who had not yet learnt to speak were showing an adult something, and, in this communication without language, were asking, with the merest inflection of its voice, 'Have you seen it?' and then affirming, again with its voice, 'I have seen it!'

But the kokil itself was invisible, apparently bodiless, for though Sandeep and his cousins chased the insistent cry from tree to tree, they found it was impossible to catch a glimpse of the bird. It did not seem to exist at all, except the cry, which rose questioningly and affirmatively again and again from the leaves. They went upstairs to tell Chhotomama about it.

'Baba!' said Abhi to his father, who was lying in bed, talking to Sandeep's mother. 'We heard the kokil today. It's got a funny voice and it keeps singing all the time.'

'Have you seen it?' asked Chhotomama.

'No, Baba. We tried to, but we couldn't.'

'Go back and look for it,' said his father. 'And when you've seen it, come and tell me what it looks like.'

It sounded like a directive in a myth or a fable, the old king ordering his son to bring him the fruit of wisdom, or Hercules being set his most difficult and hopeless task. The three boys went downstairs and searched in the garden. In an hour, they had completely forgotten about their mission, until Abhi saw the kokil accidentally while playing hide-and-seek—he had gone to the furthest end of the garden to find a place to conceal himself, when, looking up aimlessly at a tree, he had noticed it sitting on one of the higher branches, tearing a gulmohur flower with its beak. The tree was bare compared to the others,

so that the bird could be observed quite easily: it had a slim, ink-black body, and a long, attenuated tail; it gave an overall impression of shapeliness and stateliness. Abhi beckoned urgently to the others:

'This must be it,' he whispered, pointing up.

'What?' asked Sandeep.

'Look . . .' said Abhi.

Sandeep looked up. Then he understood.

'It's as black as a crow,' he said in awe. 'But much nicer-looking.'

'It's eating the orange flower,' whispered Abhi.

But it must have sensed their presence, because it interrupted its strange meal and flew off—not flew off, really, but melted, disappeared, from the material world. As they watched, a delicate shyness seemed to envelop it, and draw a veil over their eyes.

# Stories

# A Road in Late March

The road was long and wide and important. Shops, chemists, jewellers and cinemas dotted its sides. It was divided in the middle by tramlines which ran on raised ground.

When digging began all over Calcutta for the construction of the underground railways, most of this road was temporarily ruined. No one went to those shops or cinemas any more; they too were closed. As work progressed, hills of rubble rose in front of the facades of buildings, some of which were seventy or eighty years old. An outcast society, comprised of destitutes and homeless workers and refugees from the '71 war, built their homes—homes that consisted of burnt utensils and plastic sheets—on the abandoned edges of the tramlines. After ten years, when the underground was more or less

complete, the road was opened for use again, the shops resumed business as if nothing had happened, and that illusory society disappeared effortlessly.

One section of the road, however, remained closed, cut off by a small but significant mountain of rubble. A church stood here with big pillars and a lonely crucifix on its roof. It resembled a stage prop. An old man sat all day cleaning his ear in front of a deserted petrol pump. The glass windows of some empty shops, which had once sold provisions, held irrelevant reflections. There were one or two silent houses in which people lived silently. Magically, at one point this stretch ended, and the noise of the city began again.

A couple had been standing here for some time in the shadow of a disused bus stop made of two short stone escarpments and a flat stone roof. There was graffiti on the walls; bold Bengali alphabets leaping like acrobats. The two were quite alone. Cars on the other side passed continually, but that was a different world.

Finally, as if breaking a silence, the woman said:

'I'm glad it's a cloudy day.' She looked up at the sky; not much of it was visible. 'It might rain.'

A dog walked by with slow, yawning strides. It went onto the deserted road and lowered itself in a curled and comfortable heap in the faded parchment

light of the cloudy day. It was the end of March, but a surprisingly cool wind was blowing. The man, his hair rising suddenly from his forehead with the breeze, and staying back in casual, amused dishevelment after the breeze had died, said to the woman:

'Let me read your palm.'

The woman shook her head from side to side, not as a denial, but to denote grown-up amazement. He persisted:

'Sumita, show me your hand.'

A circle of people had gathered in front of the church; not the devout, but just some curious people watching something—perhaps a tantric sadhu performing a feat. There were plenty of tantrics about, bearded bare-chested men in old saffron dhotis with begging-bowls in their hands and marks on their foreheads; Kalighat and its Kali temple were nearby. One of them was perhaps now meditating in front of the church. The woman giggled and gave him her hand from beneath the sari; it peered out like a tiny living creature. He held it and seemed to weigh it; then he turned it and gazed at the palm, whose colour was pitched at an elusive glass-thin lightness. She had crumpled it into a flower; he straightened out the unwilling fingers. She was now looking at her hand as if she hadn't seen it before.

'I see,' he said in a low, disbelieving voice, 'property, wealth, and a short devoted husband.'

She squealed with laughter and tried to withdraw her hand. But he held firm without hurting her.

'Three daughters,' he said.

'*Three* daughters?' she asked. Arranging her eyebrows into an expression of concern, she said, 'Where does it say that?'

He pointed at the puzzled wrinkles on the side of her palm. He touched three faint slashes with affection.

'One, two, three,' he whispered.

Her arm was smoother and darker than his. Strands of hair ran across his arm in perfect obedient grooves.

'Tell me about,' she said softly, 'myself.'

'Yourself?' he asked, gazing deeply. He hummed a tune; 'Yourself?' He straightened the fingers that kept bending automatically.

'You have a kind heart,' he said. 'You think too much.' A calm breeze searched them out.

'You give way in arguments,' he said a little later. Then once more he scrutinized the palm carefully.

'This mound,' he said, curiously caressing its pink surface, 'is high . . . the mound of Venus. You are very passionate.'

He almost expected her to say, 'O be quiet!' at this

point, but he looked up to see that she was looking at him and listening like a child. He was aware that she was leaning on him slightly, a tiny but endlessly suggestive fraction of her weight resting on his.

She withdrew her hand abruptly.

'Enough,' she said. Then, to make up, she asked, smiling:

'What does it say in yours?'

'Oh the usual,' he replied in a mournful voice. 'Employment, retirement, death.'

'Tapan!' she exclaimed.

A breeze made dust rise dreamily from the dug-up places and form a screen around them. Their hands involuntarily shaded their eyes. Immediately the dust settled, and the cars and buildings on the other side were again visible.

'Should we cross over for a cup of coffee?' he asked.

She glanced at her wristwatch. It was a seventeen-jewel Favre-Leuba whose tiny key she wound religiously every morning. The brown band circled and clasped her wrist possessively.

'All right,' she said, glancing up, not at him, but at the sky.

They came out, two unexpected figures, from the shelter of the bus stop. They did not speak as they walked onto the abandoned road and crossed the tramlines

to the other side where normal life unfolded its self-repeating secrets. They joined the current of casual strollers on the pavement; they became invisible. On this side, the bus stop remained as before, shadowy and geometric. The dog was still sleeping. The church with its lonely crucifix, the petrol pump, the houses, the empty provisions shops, composed a queer transitional setting. Time stood still in it, as in a masterpiece.

# Lakshmi Poornima Night

It was two o'clock in the afternoon, late October. My mother lay on the large square bed; she was resting after lunch. The door and the windows of the room were closed; the air-conditioner was humming distantly, imitating the sound of a gentle precipitation; rain falling on the tin roof of a village house; if you closed your eyes as my mother had, and listened, you would be back in that village on a wet July day.

A maidservant was daubing cream and oil on my mother's feet. From time to time, she glanced at the giant glass doors on her left, beyond which you could see the roofs of bungalows, the Calcutta School of Music, the main road at Ballygunge, and beyond that, places whose names I'm not familiar with. There are several trees in this lane; sometimes you might notice

parrots flying. Above the steady murmur of the air-conditioner, there rose occasionally the clumsy but clear notes of a scale being practised on the piano in the music school. The maidservant, Savitri, was sitting on the carpet, one knee raised in a pyramid beneath her sari. Her arms, her neck and her shoulders were dark-brown and polished, like the wood on some of our doors. She went on massaging my mother's feet, moving not only her arms but her whole body as she did so; the cheap pink glass bangles around her wrist said softly: chuk-a-chuk-a-chuk-a-chuk. Her fingers tenderly stroked a deep, radiating scar on my mother's right foot.

'Ma,' she said, for she called my mother 'Ma' as I did, 'what happened here?'

'Where?' asked my mother, who had been trying to fall asleep, but hadn't.

'Here, Ma,' she said, caressing the scar.

'Car accident,' said my mother sleepily.

Savitri took in a deep, hissing breath, a sound of pain and wonder. Again she stroked the scar and the damaged bone that had healed miraculously many decades ago.

'Savitri,' said my mother.

'Ma?' she said.

'You can go now.'

'No it's all right, I'll stay another five minutes,' said Savitri.

She had a soft, hoarse voice.

'No, go now,' said my mother.

'It's all right I'll stay,' she said.

After five minutes, Savitri carefully screwed on the tops of the bottles of cream and oil and put them on the dressing-table. She folded two hankies and two blouses and one pyjama that had been lying on a chair and laid them, one on top of the other, neatly, on another chair. The folded, naked garments oozed a kind of gratitude when she touched them. She was a very good worker, perhaps a little too sweet-tongued, a little insincere in her willingness. 'You must watch her,' a neighbour had told my mother. 'She may be a thief—not big things, just little ones; knick-knacks; a pen—though a pen can be expensive.' She also might be a part-time prostitute— difficult to tell. There was an independence about her, something in her movements.

'Savitri,' I said. I had been reading a book on the rocking-chair.

'Yes, dada?' She was putting a chair, which had been out of place, into place.

'Will you give me a cup of coffee before you leave?'

'Yes, dada,' she said, not raising her face to look at me. She went out of the room.

My mother could not sleep; she kept turning from side to side. Once she opened her eyes and stared at me in an unconvinced and surprised way and then again closed her eyes. I closed the book I had been reading and laid it on my lap and said:

'Ma, I'm taking the car to College Street.'

She made no reply. Savitri came in to take my empty coffee cup. As I was about to leave, my mother said:

'When will you be back?'

'In an hour.'

'Tell Savitri,' she said, 'to take the oranges.'

'All right,' I said.

'And give her twenty rupees.'

Though I did not know which oranges my mother was referring to, I told Savitri to take them. I gave her a twenty-rupee note. In the morning she had said to my mother, hiding her body shyly behind a door, her head peering out angularly from behind it:

'Ma, give me twenty rupees.'

'Speak loudly,' said my mother, who was wearing a sari after her bath.

'Twenty rupees, Ma,' she said a little loudly.

My mother arranged the sari around her in intimate, systematic folds, the front gathering itself, pleat after pleat, like the whorls of a delicate and immense flower, the end hanging over her shoulder, innocent and limp as an elephant's trunk. It was a complex feat, like trying to open and close, at the same instant, a Japanese fan. Savitri came up to her and silently helped her adjust the tiny tributary folds.

'I gave you two saris for Durga Puja a week ago,' said my mother.

Savitri did not reply at once. She smoothed invisible undulations on my mother's sari. Then she said:

'Today is Lakshmi Puja.'

'What can I do if it is Lakshmi Puja?' asked my mother with an astonished laugh. This is an act she has perfected, of refusing or being unable to understand before she gives in as usual to the demand. The questions and answers are a game; like the measured dipping and rising of a see-saw. Again Savitri did not reply. Then she offered a solution:

'Deduct it from my salary.'

'Naturally,' said my mother. 'Oh go now leave me in peace! Every few days ten rupees, twenty rupees! Savitri go now!'

'I'm going, Ma,' she said.

As I was leaving, I saw Panna the sweeper drifting about in the hall. He comes at midday to clean the toilets. I had seen him today rigorously scrubbing a wash-basin with a rag, scouring its valley, skimming its plateau, rubbing and kneading the knobs on the taps. He goes from room to room with a bucket and a jhadu, a broom made from the firm, fine lashes of a coconut tree, which splay in bunched, pointed needles at the end like a punk's hair. He cleans the commodes with Harpic liquid, which has been recently introduced to India bearing the legend, INTERNATIONAL TOILET CLEANER.

Panna cannot keep a job for more than a month. In our house too, his position is precarious rather than entrenched. He has a thin face, high cheekbones, and a pencil-thin villain's moustache. He used to work once in a rich Marwari's factory; the rich Marwari had a house with many rooms, he told my mother, and it had a lake in it. Panna was made redundant after a strike. We came to the conclusion that the lake was a swimming-pool.

Panna said to me now in a quiet and bereaved tone:

'Can I go, saab?'

'Have you finished?' I asked him.

'Everything's finished,' he said.

'All the toilets?'

'All toilets,' he said. 'Commodes, basins. I cleaned the basin with new soap. I cleaned the commodes. Commodes don't flush properly, saab. This Calcutta water is not good. Tube-well water is good. Karporashen water is not good, saab. I washed the clothes. Must get new jhadu.' After having completed this list, he asked once more in an injured way: 'Saab, can I go now?'

'Yes,' I said.

He gave me an inconspicuous salaam, turned, walked a few paces, turned again. Slyly and softly he said:

'Saab, can you give me ten rupees? Today is Lakshmi Puja.'

I gave him the money.

As I approached the front door, I heard my mother calling me. I stopped and listened. Again I heard her voice. I walked back towards the bedroom.

My mother was now fully awake. She had propped up a pillow and was resting her head against it; she had a magazine in her hands. When she saw me she said:

'I forgot to tell you, but please buy an image of Lakshmi on your way back.'

I was a little surprised. My mother is not a religious person; we are not a religious family. But we had had some financial problems in the last few years; if suffering

gives us spiritual knowledge, insecurity at least makes us superstitious. I agreed that it was perhaps right to keep Lakshmi, the goddess of wealth and well-being, appeased. Though she had never wholly averted her face from us, as she did from so many people, as she had once done from my mother's family, she had displayed, lately, some displeasure of which we did not know the source.

'I want to do a little puja in the evening,' said my mother.

When I went downstairs, I saw all the cars parked in the shadows of trees. The watchman was leaning back on his stool, talking to the istriwalla, or The Man Who Owns An Iron, who was unfolding and ironing a white garment on his tall wooden box. The drivers of the inactive cars had congregated to play cards under a tree. They were squatting on the ground; they had spread their chequered handkerchiefs to sit on. I could see the cards of the players whose backs were turned to me. In one or two cars, the drivers were asleep, their legs raised on the dashboard or on the steering-wheel in alarming positions. One was listening to a film-song on a transistor radio. The notes of the song emanated from a dark space in his lap.

My driver was asleep in the car. He is a Muslim; his name is Sultan. I tried to open the door at the back. Sultan leapt from the seat like Houdini, his eyes red, his mouth, impossibly, smiling, his right arm darting back expertly to unlock the door.

'Where to, saab?' he asked when I had entered.

'College Street,' I said. 'And, Sultan, on the way back, I want to buy a Lakshmi thakur.'

'Oh yes, saab,' he said. 'Kalighat Bridge—many, many Lakshmis over there. Many many goddesses.'

Having said this, Sultan began to drive very fast towards College Sreet. He employed the steering-wheel and the horn with pioneering passion. Though he is an extremely charming man, Sultan reserves his most telling satire for passers-by and fellow-drivers; when pushed, he accuses them of incest. He took me through wonderful, unheard-of short-cuts; of all things he hated, he hated distance the most.

When we left the gates of Presidency College behind, I knew we had come to College Street. On either side, the pavements were lined with tiny bookstalls. As I got off, the keepers of some of the stalls began to shout to me, 'Come here, dada, which book do you want, I have the book!' Their cries pursued me, pathetic and enticing and subliminally dangerous; I was sure that if I turned

something terrible would happen; perhaps I would turn into a pig or a stone. They all called me 'dada', which means 'elder brother', though I think they were all older than me, the oldest being around seventy.

Once a man stepped in my way and held my sleeve. He said, 'Tell me which book you want, dada, I'll give it to you'; his tone was challenging. I looked at his tiny bookstall, the size of a wardrobe, stacked with books like *Basic Engineering* and *Answers To Question Papers On Econometrics*. I did not think it likely that he would have the book I wanted. I said, to ward him off:

'Do you have *Walden* by Thoreau?'

'Tho-ro, wal-den,' repeated the man slowly. 'No,' he decided, 'not that one,' glaring at me as if I had insulted him.

Another name occured to me, a rich wonderful name fit for a Theban play.

'Marcus Aurelius?'

'No no, we don't have those.' We had no more to say to each other; we had reached a kind of stunted understanding. I walked on.

Later, I bought a half-price edition of the *Complete Novels of Jane Austen* from an old man. On the way back, we stopped at Kalighat Bridge. It is a gay place,

with the expressionless facade of the Alipore Jail on one side, and prostitutes wearing bright saris on the other, standing by a shop in which men mend and make musical instruments, mainly tablas, all day. The prostitutes leered; the instrument-makers ignored them. They are true craftsmen, devotees of Vishwakarma, the god of work and industry. I have seen them opening the tabla like a gourd, listening for the resonance.

To rival the prostitute's cheap eminence were, across the road, a thousand idols of Lakshmi. They were made of clay and varied in size, but were identical in appearance. Lakshmi sat on a lotus dressed in a vermilion sari, her white owl to her left; in the curve of her left arm rested a golden container that held riches, and in the fingers of her right hand was a flower. On her head she wore a crown. She was smiling.

I did not like the idols. The images were not traditional: Lakshmi resembled a marriageable middle-class Bengali girl, an only daughter, docile and not strikingly intelligent and never hungry, spoilt and terrorized in turns by a father who has missed all his promotions, a girl who never looks at men in public, and in private is petted by a boyfriend after dark at Deshapriya Park during the time she is supposed to be at her painting class. She was plump; her cheeks

were pink as Ganguram's yoghurt. I went searching, among the deities that mirrored each other, for the right Lakshmi, the decent one. I searched for the right smile—a maternal smile, a cool, spiritual smile, like the Buddha's, even a Mona Lisa smile—but found only after-dinner smirks on their faces.

The line of idols stretching out of sight vaguely reminded me of queues outside a Hindi cinema on a Sunday afternoon. Just as I was losing hope, I saw her: it was a matter of chance. She looked like the others, but, by accident or design, her body was slender and her face beautiful. She was really smiling. It was a serene smile, and a little mocking now, because she knew I had recognized her.

I told a little excited boy—

'Give me that one.'

'Which one?' he asked, in a voice that was husky with shouting. An older man said in a bearish, threatening tone: 'Give saab the image he wants.'

I pointed at Lakshmi. But he could not see her. 'This one?' he asked, tapping a smug idol that was sitting nearby, 'Or this one?' tapping the next one, 'This one?', and then 'This one?' he asked, tapping my Lakshmi, and I said, 'Yes, that one.'

I paid the boy five rupees. I put her in the car in the

back seat, where she looked elegant and comfortable, and Sultan took us home.

It was evening. My mother had placed Lakshmi near the giant glass windows in her bedroom. The room was cool; the air-conditioner hummed in our ears. She had lit two incense sticks. With white rice paste, she had painted a pattern on the floor, in front of the idol.

'Come and see,' she said to me. 'Come and see Lakshmi's footprints.'

I came and looked.

'She walks placing one foot in front of another, as a bride does,' I said.

Then I asked:

'They lead towards her, but why don't they lead away?'

'Oh,' said my mother, 'when Lakshmi enters a house, we don't allow her to leave.'

175

Small lamps had been lit in the verandahs to welcome her; the flames looked strange and dreamlike against a background of electric light.

'How sad,' said my mother, 'if Lakshmi were to leave—we would become poor.'

'See, it is a full moon tonight,' she said after a while. 'Look—see the Poornima moon.'

I turned to the great windows; it was true; a circle of light, and around it, for miles, a ghostly radiance, an effluence. My mother laughed softly:

'You can steal if you want tonight. It's a custom. What you steal on Lakshmi Poornima night becomes yours. Of course,' she smiled, 'it's easy to spot thieves in the light of the full moon.' I saw a village asleep, and two boys, naked but for dhotis, moonlight making their shoulders bright, smuggling fruit from someone else's garden. 'Quiet, quiet,' said one boy to another. A twig snapped. A dog began to bark.

The door opened, and Rehman entered the room. He is our cook. He sleeps all day, eats plenty of rice, and wakes up at evening to cook our dinner. He has the red, glazed eyes of a drinker, but he swears he does not drink, he cannot bear to pronounce the word, his eyes have been like that from birth. His belly, beneath his tight vest, is like a distended tumour. When he

sleeps, it almost looks spiritual, a round Islamic dome covering a mosque. Once I found him standing on our weighing-machine. Before I could object, he asked me: 'What is my weight, dada?' He is illiterate, but he can read numbers; at present, however, his belly was in the way. I bent down and said: 'Eighty kilograms.' He now bowed imperceptibly before Lakshmi. My mother asked:

'Do you believe in her, Rehman?'

Rehman made a brave and titanic gesture.

'So what if I am a Mussalman, memsaab,' he said, smiling with all his stained teeth. 'Who cannot believe in Lakshmi?'

He is a great liar. A scurrilous expression came to his face and passed; his eyes shone cunningly from their alcoholic haze. He patted his belly unconsciously and made a little speech.

'All gods are one,' he said. 'Allah, Jesu, Ram . . . Memsaab, I believe in them all. After Ramzaan I eat biryani, on the Big Day I bow to Jesu, and on Durga Puja I eat khichdi.' My mother and I glanced at each other knowingly; for all of Rehman's metaphors and faiths end in food.

When I went out to the hall I found that Rehman had made lamps out of bottle-tops and arranged them in the balcony. Many of these had been extinguished by

177

the October breeze. The low houses of Ballygunge were surrounded by different trees. The moment contained, within it, the Poornima moon. I thought of the boys in that imaginary village with the stolen fruit in their hands; it was theirs now, according to the old custom. Rehman came to me from the shadows and said in his oddly malicious way: 'It's a lovely night.'

# The Happiest Man
# in the World

For the last thirty years, he had lived in London. He had been a manager in a shipping company before he retired. He had acquired nothing—not a family, or a house, or a car. He pretended to despise these things. He had been living in the bedsit he had rented as a student, until the Council bought the house and shifted him to another place temporarily, because the ceiling of the bedsit was crumbling.

Nothing disturbed him.

'Nothing disturbs me,' he said, 'if I have a cigarette and a book of ghost stories.'

He was an impossible man. He had been sending money to relatives in India for two decades; a Pakistani

neighbour, who had always been jobless and was perhaps a spy, borrowed money from him constantly.

At first, he had lived in that bedsit in Belsize Park. My parents had also lived there before I was born, when my father was a student. The three had been inseparable.

I liked Belsize Park, the adjoining Belsize Village, the church and the school. Often, at a certain time, I would see schoolchildren waiting to cross at a zebra-crossing. The first time I went to England on holiday, I was beglamoured; it was late September, and dry leaves were lying on the pavement to my uncle's house; with infinite patience, I crushed the leaves with my feet, listening to the crackle. Most of all, I liked the name of the place—Belsize Park—just as I liked all names that I read on the map in the tube station: Golders Green, Primrose Hill, Elephant and Castle, names that were either alliterative or conjured up a strangely pastoral London, or like the last, were simply fabulous and mythical, and brought to my mind's eye a castle with an elephant dancing in front of it, an image almost as hallucinatory as a cow jumping over the moon. Oxford Circus, I found, was actually a circus, where enthusiastic shoppers of every race examined garments and watches and chocolates, where pale white urchins lounged by dustbins, where nude mannequins stared from display

windows, where blue policeman strolled past bar-boys, where blind men played mandolins and white-haired Scotsmen in kilts blew on bagpipes, where ten-pence coins and rust-coloured two-pence coins heaped up in open guitar cases, and large puffy-eyed men who refused to give street directions and answered questions with a straightforward rudeness hawked copies of the *Evening Standard* standing behind wooden boxes that always had a headline pasted on them.

My uncle now lived in Chalk Farm. It would have to be a surprise visit, because he had no phone. But as I was approaching the house he saw me through a window; he had been standing in front of the mirror, which was next to the window, shaving; he had woken up half an hour ago. It was one o'clock in the afternoon. He welcomed me loudly and came to open the door in a dark maroon dressing-gown, the lather white on parts of his face.

They had put him in Room 13. It was the second room after the door of the entrance. The first room had a sign saying PLAYROOM, in which each letter of the word had been shaded in a different colour with a felt-pen. In the bland council-owned house, these colours somehow looked desperate. Every door (there were many rooms and, I think, two floors above this one) was painted a light red; the walls were a dull, uniform white.

The linoleum floor in the corridor had an alternation of red and white squares. Any attempt at imagination had been calculatedly suppressed. The old house at Belsize Park had had foul curry smells and broken bannisters. Here, everything was kept remarkably clean by a mysterious, council-paid agency.

My uncle took me into his room and began to talk: He had a lot of things to say. Living alone gave him a lot of time to think; he now wanted to air his various grievances, complaints, observations, reflections, fears. We had met three months ago and had had an argument on an absurd subject which I had now forgotten about; he resumed the argument where we had left off. I was in the dark for a few moments; then I too resumed the argument. In this sense, we have only been holding one conversation interrupted by gaps; the gaps range from ten minutes to one and a half years. Sometimes I am just silent and let him talk; he is under the impression, however, that we are holding a dialogue.

He loved hearing the sound of his own voice. It was a deep, powerful voice; it was more an African than an Indian voice. His favourite animals were the tiger and the lion; he could not decide which he liked better. He could talk about them for hours. So there must have been something of the African in him.

When I was a student in London, I had once rented a TV, and he used to visit me and sit in front of the television manically changing channels on the remote-control box. I thanked God that there weren't more than four channels. The only time he stopped to watch was when they were showing an automobile commercial on ITV or Channel 4—it was not the car he was watching, but the lion that it was being compared to. The lion was shown running, leaping, and resting. It was a magnificent creature. My uncle's eyes would widen to ping-pong balls with something like love. But the commercial lasted for not more than two minutes.

After talking continuously to me for half an hour, he excused himself to go to the toilet. I roamed around restlessly in his tiny room, pausing to look at the books on his table: fifteen copies of the *Pan Book of Horror Stories*, each with a ghastly face on the cover; Wild West books by Louis L'Amour; several murder mysteries; a book about the astral planes; one about flying-saucers and life on other planets; another about life after death. One such book and a cigarette, said my uncle, was equivalent to heaven.

A saucepan and a pot and a frying-pan were placed on the cooker. One contained rice, another chicken, and another an instant soup made from some concentrated

powder. Before going to the toilet, my uncle had again and again urged me to eat something, but I had refused. He himself could subsist till dinner-time on two cups of coffee, half a toast, and a spoonful of honey. His dietary habits were strange, like those of people who have lived all their life in the desert. I presumed that living alone in a room for so many years had made his body adapt its needs and functions to its surroundings.

In his old Belsize Park bedsit, where he did not have a fridge, he told me that he could cook something and keep it in the pan and it wouldn't go bad for ten days. It could be that his room, from being so tiny and musty and stuffy, so unentered, had a special Egyptian atmosphere in which the food, embalmed in its own sauce, was somehow kept from decay. In that room, Christmas cards—some sent by my father in the late Sixties—were pinned to the wall, and important telephone numbers were scribbled in pencil on the ancient wallpaper. On a mantelpiece that looked like a ledge, he had kept pictures—each the size of a playing-card—of different Hindu gods and goddesses, and one of the Madonna. Every evening, he performed a little Hindu ceremony, dusting the ledge with a hanky (thus the ledge was the only clean place in the room) and placing prasad, or sacred offerings, before the deities. The prasad mainly

consisted of chocolates. For his gods, he usually chose either Cadbury's or Yorkies. On his bedside-table, he had an old lamp with an elephant-shaped stand: he called this Ganesh, after the elephant-headed Hindu god of Success. This too he used to dust affectionately, like an old woman, in the evenings.

That was the Belsize Park bedsit. In the Chalk Farm room, I did not see the elephant-shaped lamp which he called Ganesh, nor the playing-card pictures of the gods and of Madonna. They must have been there somewhere. After a while, I went out to walk in the corridor with its white walls and red and white squares. Every room was silent, except the last room at the other end. Here, someone was listening to heavy rock music: the sound of electric guitars, bass guitar, lead guitar, drums, and a cracked voice trying to pronounce the lyrics of the song. Two chords were being played again and again. The noise brought to my mind a series of swift, intermingling images: an iron and steel factory in which men work twenty-four hours, a cement mixer, the whirring mechanism of a watch amplified a thousand times.

I walked away. Two women were coming down the stairs, talking, and I paused. They came into the corridor, a plump, middle-aged lady with a pleasant face, and a

185

slim young girl who also had a pleasant face. Both of them smiled, and I smiled back. They did not seem to belong here, to the rows of tiny rooms and the room with the rock music; they must be the people who came from outside and pinned up the pleasant PLAYROOM signs.

'Hello,' said the plump lady.

'Hello,' I said.

'Do you live here?' she asked, smiling, not wishing to pry. The other girl smiled.

'No,' I said. I was smiling too. 'I've come to visit my uncle. He lives in that room,' I said, pointing to his room.

'Oh!' said the plump lady. 'Oh!—is he all right?—I'm the Health Officer, you see,' she said, 'and I've been going round from room to room, but nobody seems to be there! This,' waving at the girl, 'is a nurse from the Middlesex Hospital.' As an afterthought, she said, 'We come here every month, but nobody seems to be there today.' We all smiled again, as if she had said something funny.

'My uncle's all right,' I said.

'Is he old?' the plump lady asked conspiratorially.

'Pardon?' I asked.

'Is he—how old is he?' she asked. 'I mean, is he quite old?'

'Around sixty-five,' I said.

'Oh *that's* not too old!' she said, giving me a reprimanding smile. 'I mean, that's not *old!*'

'No,' I laughed. 'At least he doesn't show it.'

The plump lady laughed loudly. She had found that last line very witty. Or possibly she was just a very happy person, the type that draws the letters of PLAYROOM in eight different colours. Then she became serious again.

'Do you visit him often?' she asked.

'Often . . .' I thought to myself. 'Not often . . . You see, I don't live in London. 'I'm a student—at Oxford.'

'Oxford!' said the plump lady, looking at the slim girl and nodding, her eyes large. 'He's come a long way, hasn't he?'

I laughed.

'Oxford!' said the lady. 'No, you can't visit too often from Oxford! The fares must be very high.'

'Quite reasonable,' I said. 'Just three pounds by coach.'

'Three pounds by coach!' said the plump lady, looking at the slim girl. 'Oh that's quite reasonable!'

'Still, I often go for my holidays to India,' I said. 'Which hardly leaves me time to come to London.'

'Yes,' she said understandingly. 'And what are you studying at Oxford?' she asked, almost winking at me.

'English,' I said.

187

'English!' said the lady to the slim girl. 'He *has* come a long way, hasn't he?'

We all laughed, the Health Officer, the nurse, and I, the Indian who had come a long way. They turned to leave.

'Bye bye,' said the plump lady. 'Will you teach English when you go back to India?'

'Don't know,' I said vaguely.

'Bye bye,' she said, closing the door and smiling her broadest smile. 'Hope you enjoy picking up our terrible English expressions!'

I smiled and waved at her. I realized she thought I had come to Oxford to learn how to speak and read and write in English.

When my uncle had finished his toilet, we went out. He had to do his weekend shopping, he said. It was not the weekend. But there is always some hidden logic in his statements, so I did not question him.

We walked up Haverstock Hill towards Belsize Park.

'Which side would you like to walk on?' he asked, suddenly stopping.

'Does it matter?' I asked.

'Well, *this* side is colder, and the other side is warmer.'

'Oh,' I said. 'Let's cross then—to the warmer side.'

We crossed and continued our walk. He was dressed in the clothes he always wears when he goes out: a three-piece suit which is out of date, and seems a little small for him, a black summer overcoat, his feet in sneakers.

'Be careful you don't step on the excrement,' he said. 'London is the dirtiest city in Europe, dog-shit everywhere.'

When we reached Belsize Park, we entered a supermarket in which cryogenized meats and packed vegetables were arranged on racks. Later we went to a post office, and from there to a tea-shop in Hampstead tucked beneath the hill between two rising roads, where we had coffee and sausage rolls. He went on talking lugubriously about his pension and inflation, and of a heart-chilling time in the future when ten thousand pounds would be equivalent to today's four hundred pounds, perhaps forty pounds.

'The problem with me,' he said, 'is that I'll live till I'm hundred—probably hundred and twenty.'

He was worried about himself, heirless, and about how he would send money to his relatives in India. He paused to say a few nasty things about his relatives, who were also my relatives. I scolded him. He scolded me, and ordered another coffee for me. 'Have another sausage roll?' he asked paternally. I shook my head.

The discussion turned theological, and he began to say nasty things about existence. He said some terrible things about God. He had once composed a poem which began, 'God—You are an idiot.' The thesis of the poem was that God had made a mess of Creation. He now quoted from the poem. I said, 'Why don't you return to India?' 'I can't stand Indians,' he said. 'Stupid, oily, cow-eyed creatures. They'll leave me destitute, and I won't be able to stop them.' Then he said, 'I wish people would stop bothering me. I know why people back home want to see me—for them, it's like going to the circus. Well, I don't want to see anyone. I wish they'd stop bothering me.'

'What exactly do you have against going back?' I persisted. 'What do you have here?'

'Have against going back?' he said. 'I can't go back. Everyone has his own life. I want to return to everyone living in the same place, and sitting in the evening in the same room, as we used to do in Shillong. Everyone with enough money to live on—not rich or poor—just enough money to live on comfortably. Sitting and talking in the same room in the evening—everyone—Sejdi, Mejda, Dukhu, Ranji, Khaku, Boudi, Monji . . .'

'That's silly,' I said. 'It's impossible.'

'Let's not talk about it,' he said.

My visit was ending. He came to drop me at Marble Arch. It was suddenly cold in March. We searched for the lavatory among the great underground maze around the tube station. We found it at last, clean and empty and gleaming. A row of white urinals faced us. As he urinated, my uncle talked about life and his childhood. All his stories and memories were sad. His voice echoed among the clean white urinals.

We came up the stairs to the bus station. My uncle could not stand saying goodbye, so he shuffled around uneasily, repeating one gloomy story after another. He was going bald, and he had taken to cutting his hair himself. This winter, he had decided to grow his hair long, so that it stuck out on all sides like tiny black quills.

'You must get a haircut,' I said, looking at him.

'Yes,' he replied a little sheepishly. 'It's bad, isn't it?'

'It's quite bad.'

There was silence for some time; then I said:

'Have you no happy stories? I'm tired of listening to these grumbling, complaining, snivelling stories— they have no dignity. Anyone can tell a sad story—two estranged lovers, a man who lost a leg or a life, a child who lost his parents. But it's difficult to tell a happy story.'

His eyes lit up.

'Oh, happy stories? No end of happy stories! If it's happy stories you want . . . '

A queue was waiting for the bus to Oxford. No one, thankfully, was listening to us.

In the first story, my uncle was seven years old. The family, made of seven brothers, two sisters, and a widowed mother, lived in Sylhet. It was about how my uncle had wandered alone to see the hills at the end of the town, passing through a street in which the strange, bearded Mussalmans lived. The second story was about the delight my uncle had felt, when he was three years old, in demolishing a new 78 rpm record. The third story I liked the best, so I record it in full. It is about the happiest man in the world. When my uncle was around seven, there was a big clock in the house. My uncle used to gaze at the clock every day, hands on hips, dreaming only one dream: he longed to touch the black hands of the clock behind the glass cover on its face. If there is such a thing as the joy of touch, said my uncle, it was to be known by touching the hands behind the glass. Each day my uncle spent some time pondering over this problem. Then, one day, he saw the happiest man in the world. He was wearing a dhoti and a shabby shirt, and had black stubble on his face. He was standing on a

ladder; he had opened the glass cover, and was touching the black hands of the clock with his fingers. He was the watch-repairer. My uncle was overwhelmed by this vision of perfect peace and joy.

Around this time, the Citylink bus to Oxford arrived at the bus stop. Its doors opened automatically; it waited for the queue to enter; it was an extremely polite and well-behaved machine.

'Those were wonderful stories you told me,' I said. 'Do you have any more?'

'Many more,' said my uncle. He shivered suddenly.

'Will you come to Oxford next week?' I asked. 'You can spend the night in the room.'

'I'll try,' he said. 'Don't think so—you know my routine—but I'll try.'

I boarded the bus. I was the last in the queue.

'Try your best,' I said. 'If not, I'll see you soon anyway!'

'Okay!' he said.

The doors closed automatically. I waved at him through the glass. Then I went up and sat next to a window. I could see him from upstairs, but he was searching for my face among the faces downstairs. The bus moved forward.

# Jadav

In the morning, after eating breakfast and reading the newspaper, the boy went to the bathroom and opened the hot water and cold water taps—small, stylish, silver-coloured knobs with indentations—and extended his hands beneath the faucet. The knobs however began to vibrate, and water trickled from their sides. He screwed them shut and opened them again. Water poured from the faucet, but the silver-coloured knobs hummed contentedly in a deep baritone; then, getting a little louder, they began to broadcast curious orchestral sounds.

Disgusted, the boy kept the taps running and went to the kitchen. Jadav, the servant, a thin young man in pyjamas, was sitting on a stool in front of the fridge, picking his teeth with a matchstick.

'How many times have you been told,' said the boy, 'to wear a shirt in the house. Is this a village?'

Jadav sheepishly got up from the stool. He swung one arm shyly. The bright tea-coloured skin was stretched upon the bones of his shoulders and his chest as lightly as a perfectly-fitting fabric; there was not an inch of extra flesh on him.

'Well?' asked the boy.

'This is not a village,' said Jadav.

'Then wear your shirt!'

Jadav disappeared into his tiny room. He emerged two minutes later buttoning a shirt with red checks.

'The other shirt has gone for wash and this one just got dry, so I thought . . .'

The boy turned to go, beckoning him with one hand to follow.

Dutifully, Jadav walked behind him with a slight stoop which he did not usually have, muttering:

'. . . so I thought if memsaab would buy me a nice cotton shirt I would not have the problem of washing one and waiting for—'

The boy stopped abruptly in the hall and turned round.

'How many months have you been working here?'

Jadav closed his parted mouth. A hunted expression came to his face. His eyes became innocent.

'Dada?' he asked.

'How many months have you been working here?' asked the boy, relentless.

'How many *months?*' asked Jadav.

'Yes, how many months,' said the boy.

'Working *here?*' asked Jadav.

'Here,' said the boy. 'Here.'

Jadav smiled suddenly, as if everything had been solved.

'Three months, dada,' he said. 'February, March, April. February 15th I joined, and today is—'

'And haven't you been told,' said the boy, 'that you get your uniform when you complete six months?'

'O yes,' nodded Jadav happily. 'Memsaab told me—When you complete six months, you get your uniform.'

'Then why do you go on and on about the shirt?' asked the boy sadly. 'Why, when we have already given you pyjamas?'

'That's right,' admitted Jadav. 'You have given me pyjamas.'

He glanced down at them in puzzlement and wonder.

'I bought them myself,' said the boy, 'from Gariahat. There are four prices—eighteen rupees, twenty-one rupees, twenty-six rupees, and twenty-eight rupees.

And I bought,' said the boy sadly, 'the pair that cost twenty-eight rupees. Best-quality cloth, the same as I buy for myself.' At this point, the boy glanced at his own pyjamas, and then at Jadav's. They were both equally white.

'Yes,' Jadav agreed, touching and teasing his pyjamas with the tips of his fingers. 'This cloth—no question about it. You can't get better cloth than this in Calcutta. So soft, like cream.'

'Then say no more about shirts,' said the boy, turning again and beginning to walk towards his room. 'We have work to do. The taps are in a mess.'

At eleven o'clock the boy was reading a book in his room when he heard a strange sound in the hall, like the crackle of electricity. Then it was gone, but no, there it was again. He closed the book and rose from the bed and opened the door and looked out. He saw a man standing on one of the dining-chairs with emerald-green covers that had oriental patterns sewn on them; he was stretching out one hand towards a light shaded with crystals that was hanging from the ceiling; the light was on, and glowed from the sides of his hand; he had laid a newspaper on the emerald-green cover of the chair, and this newspaper crackled mildly each

time he moved his feet. Jadav was standing by the chair, looking up past the man's head at the light.

At this point, the boy's father opened the door of his bedroom and came out. He said:

'Ah there you are at last! What are you doing?'

'Just checking the light, sir,' said the man on the chair, looking down and yet trying to reproduce, by a great imaginative feat, the effect that he was looking up at the boy's father. 'Giving everything a thorough check-up.'

'Good, good,' said the father. Then he said with a genuinely concerned expression on his face: 'But I can't understand the fans at all.'

'What's the matter with them?' asked the man.

'None of the regulators seem to work!' he said, apparently astounded. 'When you want the fans to turn fast, they turn slow; when you want them to turn slow, they stop turning altogether!'

The boy, who had been listening silently so far, now said decisively:

'And sometimes they go from slow to fast or fast to slow for no reason . . . Sometimes they won't even start!'

'Quite right,' said his father. 'Quite right.'

'I'll have a look at them, sir,' said the man on the chair. 'You needn't worry.'

'Ha-ha—worry? The way you people talk! I've been

chasing you for three days,' said the boy's father. 'My man Jadav went looking for you—'

'In the afternoon sun,' said Jadav.

'In the afternoon sun—three days. You come one day, disappear the next without completing your work. Once you disappear no one can get hold of you. It's astonishing! Tell me,' he asked, 'are you people ghosts, or people? No one can catch hold of you. Electricians, plumbers, all the same. Are you ghosts or what?'

'Whatever you wish, sir,' said the man on the chair. 'We are whatever you wish.'

'I wish you would fix the fans,' said the boy's father. 'But I think you are ghosts.'

At three o'clock in the afternoon, when the boy was lying on the sofa in his room, reading, two men knocked at the door.

'Yes?' said the boy.

One of them poked his head in. For some time the boy gazed at the head, apex of God's handiwork, each head as different from another as a thumbprint, in this case simply and uncomplicatedly floating without the body.

'Yes?' said the boy.

'Plumber,' said the man.

'Oh, plumber,' said the boy. 'Come in, come in.' He waved towards the bathroom door. 'The taps,' he said.

The two men came in. The first man was of medium height, around forty years old, bald, stout, with short arms. In one hand he held a cloth bag which contained tough and tensile implements. His hands and part of his forearms were white, as if he had been dipping them in talcum powder, till suddenly the white died and the brown and human river of his skin began again. The second man was younger and taller; his hands were white as well. He glanced around the room at the painting and the cupboards and the beds and the sofa, probably comparing it with other rooms he had entered that day. Shyly, like a policeman, the older man turned the brass knob on the bathroom door and opened it.

They both gazed at the basin. They whispered to each other, not so much from a desire not to disturb the boy, but, it seemed, from a wish not to break the pure crystalline calm of the bath. Sunlight fell on the pale green tiles, turning them into an edible pistachio. They approached the basin silently, with bottomless love and suspicion. The older man opened the taps. Instantly the taps began to sing—gara gara gara ga ga gara—sublime as a Russian choir. He closed the taps and plucked out one of the silver-coloured knobs like a flower; then he

bent down to gaze at where its ugly stem descended to its roots and then disappeared endlessly into the water-pipes of the building. At this point the younger man closed the door softly.

The boy tried to read, but could not. The faint but clear clinking of metal came now from the bathroom. One note rang out, echoing itself at a fixed and invariable pitch like a bird's mating call. Then another clanking sound followed, lower on the musical scale, like another bird replying from another tree. It went on in this way, making the boy think of a forest in springtime.

He laid the book aside and walked to the bathroom and opened the door. He found the older man crouched and squatting on his haunches in the shadow of the basin, surrounded by a circle of chipped concrete. He seemed quite happy there, in his cave. The other man had opened the window on the right and was ruthlessly scaring away pigeons who had made their homes among the junctions of the water-pipes outside. The pigeons were making stricken, protesting noises, protesting not at the man but at fate, which had made them pigeons, and the boy could hear the furious flapping of their wings diminishing to a single agitated wingbeat.

'How long will you take?' he asked.

The older man looked up from under the basin.

'Not long,' he said. 'Say—another fifteen minutes?'

'All right,' said the boy. 'Will you clean up before you leave?' he asked, gesturing towards the rubble.

The man gazed at it affectionately, as if it were his lunch.

'O this,' he said. 'No need to worry, dada, everything will be cleaned up by me and my man and left as it was before.'

The boy nodded and closed the door. He went out into the hall where everything was silent. He found the chair on which the electrician had stood in the morning to catch the light positioned at an angle from the others, the newspaper still covering it. He straightened the chair and folded the paper, last Friday's. Then he went to the panel of neat switches on the wall and turned on the fan tentatively. It began to spin slowly, and as he gazed at its three blades it gathered speed, and the blades disappeared into a thousand radiating tendrils—till he switched it off and it slowed down and the three blades emerged again as if after a flood. Looking down, he found that the newspaper he had put on the table had flown away quietly to a corner of the hall.

'Jadav,' he called. 'Jadav.'

There was no answer. He said loudly this time:

'Jaa—' and he broke off '—dav.'

No one. He went to the kitchen and then to the man's tiny room and found it empty, with one light burning. He switched it off. Then he opened a connecting door and went into the passage leading to the front door and found Jadav standing in the doorway in pyjamas and a white vest, smoking a beedi and talking to the janitor who was swabbing the floor outside the flat with a wet rag. In the grey sunlight that filled the rectangle of the doorway, both were figures in a framed picture.

'What's the matter, Jadav,' asked the boy, coming from behind, 'can't you hear me?'

Jadav turned and hid the beedi, holding it behind his back.

'Did you call, dada?' he asked. 'I couldn't hear you at all!'

'How could you,' said the boy, 'when you are standing here talking to this man?'

The guilty janitor made off without looking up with his bucket and wet rag. He left behind a floor which was burnished and echoed the sunlight and smelled sourly of disinfectant.

'Besides,' said the boy, 'you left the light on in your room. Have you any idea that it costs money?'

Jadav looked penitent. The telltale smoke from the

beedi began to rise in pale wisps from behind his back, where he had kept his right hand.

'Is your hand on fire?' asked the boy.

'Fire, dada?' asked Jadav. The smoke continued to rise in a fragile ladder behind his head.

'Yes,' said the boy. 'Your hand—is it on fire?'

'O no,' said Jadav. 'It's only—'

The boy shook his head from side to side and smiled. Jadav also smiled when he saw this. Jadav smiled at the boy and the boy smiled at his own thoughts. Jadav misunderstood and thought there would be a reconciliation now, it was all all right. Then the boy stopped smiling and Jadav dropped his gaze uneasily.

'Now I've forgotten,' said the boy, 'why I was calling you.'

The boy fell asleep on a sofa in the living-room. He had a dream. In the dream he and his parents had gone out. Jadav was swaggering around the house bare-bodied. He was wearing the boy's pyjamas. The two plumbers and the electrician were standing in the doorway talking to Jadav, who was however in the hall. All the lights in the hall were burning. There were no fans in the house, and the boy was telling this to Jadav although he was not at home but out with his parents.

He woke up. His throat was dry. He got up and walked to his room; he found the bathroom door closed. He opened it and saw it was empty inside. The bits of chipped concrete lay scattered on the floor as before, but everything else looked untouched. He opened the taps and once more the despondent fugue began. He closed the taps and cursed. No, they can never do anything properly, they never complete their work, who'll clean this up, the man had promised, they've left it all unfinished, where are they, thought the boy, going out into the hall and then to the living-room and then from the kitchen to Jadav's room and then from the guest-room to the room in which his parents were peacefully sleeping. Neither Jadav nor the plumbers were in the house. They're ghosts, thought the boy. Ja-dav, Ja-dav, he shouted, but not aloud, just again and again silently inside his head, so that no one heard.

# Episode Concerning a House

At midnight, the lady felt thirsty and reached across in the dark for her jug of water. Her hand encountered, in its search, an object that had the jug's artificial smoothness but not its careful roundness. Rejecting this as the table-lamp, her fingers ran enquiringly along the spine of an open book, and went from there to a blank space where the jug should have been. Here, the hand registered an absence; then it retreated with a kind of physical sob. The lady switched on the lamp.

'That boy,' she said, 'he's useless.'

'Why?' asked her husband in a voice that was far from sleep.

'Jug,' she said wearily.

The husband did not say anything. He could not

understand what she was talking about, but if he said this she might mind.

'He has not given the jug.'

'Oh,' said the husband. Wisely he added, 'He doesn't have his heart in the job.'

'No,' agreed the lady. 'It's clothes he wants—jeans, shirts. And visiting his father every weekend. I hate that father, he's like a piece of cardboard.'

Around their conversation, silence and moonlight stretched for miles. The lady rose and left her room and walked towards the kitchen with slow steps. She saw the boy sleeping in the hall, lying on the carpet beneath a fan, his mouth open. His body seemed to say, Ah how wonderful it is to lie on a hot April night in the breeze of a swiftly spinning fan, not wearing anything but a pair of cotton pyjamas. The lady entered the kitchen and switched on the tube light which flickered on and off and on and off before it came to life. In its pure blue light she opened the cupboard in which rows of clean tumblers were kept. As she picked one at random, she noticed that parts of the floor appeared to move. Peering closely (how difficult it was to see without her spectacles!) she saw tiny black cockroaches wandering all around her on the floor, out as if on a Sunday evening stroll or on a festival. They were everywhere, a constantly

changing constellation, lively and repugnant. Softly the lady put down the tumbler and switched off the light and hurried back.

'Everything,' said the lady. 'Clean everything.'

It was morning, and she was standing like a commander in the kitchen doorway, and the boy who had been sleeping with open mouth last night was crouching in front of the pantry with a wet rag and a soft jhadu.

'Lazy boy,' she said. 'You have made the kitchen filthy.' She walked up to the cooker and touched the wall behind it, stained with groundnut oil and turmeric. 'Let me see if you mention visiting your father this weekend.' The boy wrung the rag and began to scrub the wall. 'See what happens when you come to me next time asking for Pear's soap, you spoilt boy. Pear's soap!—from now on you get Lifebuoy.'

The boy thought of Pear's soap, it is dark red, and like a mirror, and you can see your hand through it, and it smells sweet. 'I don't mind,' he said. 'Lifebuoy is all right.'

'Of course it's all right!' said the lady. 'And don't answer back! The cockroaches are so confident now that they even come out in daylight!' She pointed amazedly at two cockroaches moving rapidly like businessmen

with briefcases on the narrow ledge next to the cooker. Then they ran down the sheer side of the ledge where all was darkness.

The boy said, 'Memsaab, who knows from where they come, it's amazing!'

'I know from where they come,' said the lady, full of patience, going to the dustbin filled with vegetable peelings and eggshells and fishbones and chickenbones and old rice and dal. 'This terrible dustbin, this is where they come from.' The boy came and stood next to her and gazed at the dustbin in wonder. 'No lid,' said the lady. 'That is why. I want this cleaned every day.'

'Every day,' said the boy. 'I clean it every day.'

'Don't lie,' said the lady tolerantly. 'It will get you nowhere. And every night from tonight you will spray Flit—no, not Flit, Baygon—in this kitchen.'

'Baygon,' he said, 'where will I buy it?'

The lady stared at the boy in astonishment, as she had considered the two cockroaches not long ago. 'Have I to tell you that?' she asked.

'No no,' said the boy quickly. 'There are many shops here, I will go down—'

In the afternoon the lady's husband went to Lake Market and got out from his car. He went into a shop outside the

market which had everything from buckets to cosmetics to clothes-pegs to tricycles to dolls. He asked the man behind the counter:

'Do you have a plastic dustbin?'

'Babai!' shouted the man. 'Show him the plastic dustbins!'

'With a lid,' said the lady's husband, smiling.

'With a lid!' shouted the man.

The man called Babai took the lady's husband to the left entrance of the small shop where the buckets, which were actually dustbins, had been kept. He took out one large as an African drum. He put a lid on it.

'Is there a smaller size?' enquired the lady's husband.

Now the man silently took out one the size of an ice-bucket. The husband examined each carefully, the drum and the ice-bucket, and tried to visualize how each would look in the kitchen. I wish she had told me which size she wanted, he thought to himself. Babai, meanwhile, watched his face.

'The big one is sixty-five rupees and the small one is twenty-five rupees,' he said.

The husband silently tapped the sides of the dustbin. He hummed a tune. He seemed confused but happy.

'Is there no size in between?' he asked.

'No, out of stock,' said Babai. 'The stuff comes from Bombay.'

'Then give me the big one,' he said at last. Taking out his wallet, he counted: 'Fifty, sixty, sixty-five.'

He looked at the dustbin. I wish it was a better colour, maybe I should ask if there are other colours, but after all it's only a dustbin, he thought, the colour won't matter much after a week. He lifted it with both hands and walked towards the car. People glanced at him.

In the evening, after dinner, when the lady and her husband were sitting in the hall watching yet another documentary about paddy fields on television, the boy, after having washed the dishes, began to spray Baygon in the kitchen. Strenuously he pushed the pump and then pulled it out. Each time he did so, the pump said, Shh, shh, shh.

'Mmmf!' said the lady, closing her nostrils with her fingers. 'What a smell!'

'It's you who wanted it done,' said the husband.

'We can't even watch television any more,' she said. 'Of course there is nothing to watch.'

'Nothing to watch,' he echoed.

At this point the lights went out. A pinpoint of light

shone like a perplexed star in the centre of the television, then disappeared.

'It's peculiar,' said the woman's voice in the dark. 'It just happens any time.'

'Disaster,' said her husband's voice.

'It's not getting better, it's getting worse,' she said. 'Day by day, it's worse.'

'They should publish a schedule,' his voice replied reflectively. 'Saying that at this and this time it will happen.'

From the kitchen came a whisper, Shh, shh, shh.

'The boy has not stopped,' whispered the lady, who was now gradually becoming visible. 'He will not stop till we ask him to stop.'

'Then tell him to stop,' said her husband. His voice sounded hot.

'You tell him to stop,' she said.

'Ram!' cried the husband. 'Ram!'

'Saab?' called the boy from the kitchen.

'Ram, stop,' said the husband. 'No need to do it now.'

'All right, saab,' said the boy.

They sat in the dark for some time, talking about why servants were all like this, and they decided it was because they had not eaten proteins when they were children. The air they breathed was made foul by

insecticide. Groping, they found their way to their room, but even here the smell followed them.

The cockroaches survived. Each morning the boy swept away a pile of dead ones and in the evening new cockroaches had appeared. Both the boy and the lady felt exhausted.

'Where do they come from?' she asked. She glanced at the dustbin with its lid on; it looked innocuous, like a giant pastry.

'Memsaab,' said the boy, leaning towards the kitchen window, 'they climb up the pipes from downstairs and come in through the windows.'

'Up ten floors?' asked the lady.

'O yes,' said the boy.

The lady put her head against the mullions of the window but could not see anything. She tried to visualize the cockroaches, dark-brown phosphorus-bright wings, legs like bent filaments, long, vivid antennae—obviously God hadn't made these creatures, they had existed before God existed—and she tried to imagine something like a human intelligence inside those tiny, voracious bodies.

'I can't believe it,' she said.

'O yes,' said the boy. 'The sweeper said so.'

'I'll call the pest-control,' said the lady. 'I will go out and phone!'

Their phone had not been working for three weeks. After lunch, the lady's husband got a strongly worded letter typed by a professional typist at Rashbehari Avenue; then he drove to the Calcutta Telephone Exchange in his area. A long line of people of all types and all classes, poor people, middle-class people, illiterates, teachers, old women, children, were standing in queues that led to two counters. They stood patiently in line with forms in their hands, dabbing their faces with hankies, waiting as if to catch a glimpse of a faith-healer or a saint. The lady's husband joined a queue.

'Should I cover these too?' asked the boy.

It was the day of the pest-control. The kitchen cupboards had been emptied. Everything was laid out in the hall and on the dining-table, pots, pans, dishes, tumblers, kitchen knives, jars of sugar and salt, spices, teapots, cups, saucers, cutlery, bottles, jugs, tea-strainers, things ranging from the ornamental to the most humble, old spoons, tarnished stainless steel mugs, forgotten flasks, chipped dishes with candles still on them, everything was out, all the etcetera etcetera of daily life in a household. The boy was hovering

around them, covering them with old copies of the *Statesman*.

'Of course you must cover those too,' said the lady. 'Cover them well or they'll smell for weeks.'

All the windows were closed and the curtains drawn. The lady was ready to go out; she was in a bright sari; in one hand she held a large bag which contained various knick-knacks and a fresh sari for the evening.

'I'm going to my sister's house and then to my brother's house,' she said. 'I will return with saab later. When they finish, wait for two hours and then open the windows. Keep everything back in place. Don't pull back the curtains till the sun goes down, it's bad for the carpets. You and the sweeper clean up the house later.'

'Yes, memsaab,' said the boy. He was glad to be left alone for these five hours. He felt like dancing with gladness. When he would go down to call the sweeper later, he would smoke a beedi and play a round of cards.

'Remember to clean up everything,' said the lady as she opened the front door.

'Yes, memsaab,' sang the boy, light as an angel.

The rooms and the hall were silent and empty, pregnant as a battlefield before battle.

# The New Maidservant

The new maidservant came to work in the morning. She rang the doorbell, which sounded like chimes. It was the first musical sound of the day, and was ephemerally lovely to the ear. It was Rehman who opened the door.

The lady and her husband were eating breakfast at the table. Pale light came in through the verandah and fell impartially on the table and on their faces and hands. Already the pigeons were busy, making sounds in their throats that were soft and liquid and utterly unlike any other sound.

The lady had not turned on the fan, for a mild breeze blew in through the verandah. Her husband's eyes were still a little red and the skin around them somewhat puffy. As he bit into his toast, it made an

urgent crackling sound that surprised him momentarily. In the bedroom, the bed lay unmade in the new light, last night's smothered quilt and crushed pillows lying naked in brightness.

The maidservant entered the room and began hesitantly to make the bed. She felt shy, and tip-toe on the carpet, for this was her first day. It was a beautiful flat, and to her eyes everything in it seemed to be made either of sugar or pistachio or jaggery or caramel or some fragrant, edible thing. The raised marble platform by the window would be sweet and cold as a mint lozenge if one could possibly taste it, and the dark wooden furniture would have the bittersweet taste of burnt sugar. She lifted the quilt, in which her arms sank lavishly, and folded it. She placed it on the nether end of the bed. She assaulted the pillows mercilessly till they were plump and flushed, and then placed them in reposeful postures against the bedhead.

The lady came in singing. Morning always found her bright and lively, not groggy like her husband. She was an insomniac, and was grateful when the day came. In the afternoons, she slept deeply for an hour. Her morning tea, which was weak and watery and unsweetened, a golden pool in her teacup, was enough to refresh her. The taste of weak tea she associated with morning and new

life and health and journeys. Her hair was tied in a tidy bun; the swiftness with which she had looped it—hair, that elusive but troublesome thing, so insidious and soft and so unexpectedly different from the rest of the body, synthetic, like silk—the swiftness with which she had neatly looped it into a bun also strangely uplifted her. She was wearing a light cotton housecoat made by a Parsi tailor in Bombay which she had bought here at a sale; she thought she looked a little comic in it, but it hid her feet from view, and was fluffy and energetic, and seemed to carry her along with its own motion. Though she was sixty, each day she found something that made her feel younger.

She stopped singing and hovered busily around the bed and asked:

'Your name is Meera, isn't it?'

'Yes, Ma,' murmured the maid.

'Come with me,' she said.

She took her to a cupboard; the maid followed her with downcast eyes. Outside, the light had grown harsher and simpler, and the pigeons made loud, dry noises. Even the car-horns seemed to have a definite character, quite different from twenty minutes ago; more impatient and less hopeful. Yet in the cupboard—'This is called a "bedcover",' said the lady, saying 'bedcover' in

English—the folded garments and sheets and towels on the racks lived in a twilight coolness, perfectly folded by human hands, asleep on their sides like children.

They went to the bed and the lady unfolded the bedcover with a quick movement. As she did so, the printed flowers on it seemed to wake and dance, and the maid watched anxiously, afraid they would fall onto the floor.

'See?' said the lady. 'See how beautiful it is?'

'Give it to me, Ma,' murmured the maid.

She took it in her hands, which were small and brown and hard and somehow made the lady sad, as the shy fleeting music of the coloured glass bangles around her wrist made her sad, and with a flap opened it onto the empty face of the bed. Then kindly but confusedly she began to tug and pull at it in all directions, and each time she did so, the bedcover broke out in mild, protesting waves. But the lady sighed and said:

'That isn't the way to do it. Spread it on the bed till it covers it and then stand back to see it isn't crooked. You must know how to set it perfectly, because there's nothing worse than a crooked bedcover, everything's spoilt.'

So saying, she bent forward with surprising alacrity, and in that comical bent manner went pulling and straightening with equal, exact gestures the bedcover

from the three sides of the bed. The maid watched her closely.

'See how easy it is?' said the lady, short of breath. Her face was a little red, yet triumphant. 'But it's hot!' She went and impulsively switched on the fan. As it began to turn, a piece of paper rose magically in mid-air with the breeze, and then fell to the carpet and sailed haphazardly here and there and here and there like a drunken yacht. Smiling a small smile, the maid ran after it, pursuing it a short distance across the room, till she had snatched it daringly with her fingers and brought it back and returned it solemnly to its place. 'Now you do it,' the lady was saying. 'Smooth it and tuck it in firmly so that even if someone sits on it or lies on it all day long it won't move an inch from place.' Obediently, the maid stepped forward, and adjusted the sides scrupulously for another ten minutes till she was satisfied. It was essential that she did it successfully, because, to the lady, a well-made bed was as right and natural to morning as were tea and sunlight.

In the hall, the lady's husband sat on a sofa reading a newspaper. He was wearing a pair of diminutive reading-glasses, which made him look intense and inquisitive, like a scientist. Behind his head there was a painting of

a bird that his wife had bought. It was not a particular species of bird, it was a product of the artist's fantasy, many-coloured, and yet it was not a wholly imaginary being with wings and a beak, it had an unmistakable birdness about it. During the day, with the curtains half-drawn because of the heat, and the hall a little dark like the interior of a forest or like a cloudy day, the bird seemed asleep, but at night it came alive beneath the radiant electric lights.

The lady drifted into the hall and said:

'Did you go for a walk this morning?'

'It's too hot,' said her husband.

'You don't have to go down,' she said. 'You can walk here, from the hall to the dining room to the guest room and back. You can do that for half an hour.'

The husband looked interested.

'I can do that,' he said.

'Of course you can!' she said firmly and kindly. 'I'll turn on the fans in the room, so you won't feel hot.'

'No,' he said. 'No need for that.'

He rose and began to walk. After his retirement, his doctor had told him that 'walking is good for you'. It was something to do. One must never stop doing something. He moved along with his body's rhythm. As he reached the end of the guest room, he glanced

out of the window and saw tramlines and trees and terraces of low buildings. Turning, he carried with him this glimpsed impression of Calcutta, old and vast and complicated. He felt like a character in a storybook who had gazed out for a moment in his brief, imagined life at the real world. He could easily have been a storybook character were it not for these things he constantly felt, like heat and coolness, and the dust he inhaled when he went outside, which convinced him that he was a real person with a real life. Walking back, he passed the dining table and noticed Rehman slicing something in the kitchen. He repeated this route for half an hour.

But now the new maid came into the hall with a jhadu, and bent forward and began to beat the carpet with it, so that he had to skirt round her as well as the centre table during his walk. He did not mind; it was a pleasant diversion. She was small and dark, and wore a colourless sari, but in her hair, at the back of her head, there were two red flowers singing inaudibly and celebrating themselves.

As she beat the carpet with the fine, hard bristles of her jhadu, crescent-like patterns appeared on it. Two patches of sweat had formed on her blouse around her underarms, two black moons. With a soft swishing jhadu now, she chased the dust and woolly bits of carpet to a

corner. When she looked up, she saw Rehman watching her from the kitchen.

'Would you like a cup of tea?' he asked, coming to the doorway. She paused in her work and caught her breath and said:

'Not now. In another fifteen minutes,' and smiled at him.

'I'll make you a cup of tea,' he said quickly, and moved out of view.

The lady's husband saw them from the guest room, but only imperfectly heard their exchange. He had seen the maid smile at Rehman, and had noticed how well her smile fitted her small mouth. He did not think about it; when he passed her in the dining room on his way to the hall, she had gone back to being a maid, and nothing seemed important to her but dust.

After a while, she began to swab the floor with a moist rag. The lady's husband decided he had walked long enough, for the maid always came in his path, making him feel as if he were blundering callously. He returned to his bedroom, and found his wife just emerged from the bath. She was drying her hair with a towel, and staring at the mirror, as if the world she saw in it had never been seen by her before. How young she looked!—not a day older than thirty-five.

'Have you finished?' she asked, still regarding the mirror. Even her voice sounded clean and washed with water.

'Yes,' he mumbled, and then recalled, 'My newspaper!' Unwillingly, introspectively, he turned and opened the door. Outside, a sour smell of disinfectant rose from the moist floors. The maid had turned on the fans so that the floors might dry quickly. Walking beneath the spinning fans impatiently, he encountered a sudden breeze and a sour but haunting smell.

Meanwhile, in the kitchen, the maid sighed and washed her hands at the kitchen basin.

'Don't let memsaab catch you doing that,' Rehman said.

'Why?' she asked with some irritation.

'Nothing, it's just that she doesn't like people washing in the kitchen. You have to go to the bathroom inside.' He pointed to a door on the left. The servant's bathroom was a small echoing place with clean white tiles and one electric bulb and a tap that was forever dripping. Softly he said, 'Kitchen is only meant for washing dishes.' He uttered the word 'kitchen' in English; the rest was an odd mixture of Hindi and Bengali, Rehmanspeak. This word—'kitchen'—stood out mysteriously, as if it were not only a room but a way of life.

Nonchalantly she bent to drink from her cupped palms. Then she wiped her mouth and her hands on her sari—with great delicacy, it seemed to Rehman.

'Here,' he said. 'Take your tea.'

She held the tumbler with both hands. Sitting on her haunches on a wooden stool, she crouched forward, sipping with a long and loud and satisfied sound. Rehman watched her as he dried a plate with a white cloth. His eyes ran across her neck; he barely glanced at the two flowers in her hair; her breasts were hidden by her knees; her back was curved like a line in an unfinished sketch, and her shoulders were sloped and hard.

'Do you have any bread?' she asked.

He walked to the fridge and reached for a plastic box he kept on top of it. Opening its lid with a tiny popping sound he took out two white slices and gave them to her. Folding one carefully, she dipped it in the tumbler till it was brown. It was eleven o'clock in the morning.

That afternoon, as the lady was taking a nap, she thought she heard the phone ringing. She was about to get up and answer it when she realized it couldn't be, their phone hadn't been working for a month. It must have been some vibration passing through the still afternoon air that had deceived her ear.

When she turned on her side, she saw her husband was not asleep but reading the newspaper. She wondered what it could be that he was reading. Then she thought that she must tell Rehman to sell the old copies of the newspapers that were stuffed now in two drawers in the hall. He'll be very eager to sell them, she thought grimly, and of course he'll forget to give me the money. She got irritated with him without knowing why—it was something to do with his smooth manner and red eyes and large belly; it was the big belly she resented most and felt an especial sense of rivalry with, for it seemed to ignore her sovereignty and in a sense it ruled the house. Irritated, she wondered whether Rehman had put the garbage down the garbage-chute as he was supposed to; she decided to take it up with him later. Lastly, her thoughts went to the new girl, Meera, and here her irritation changed into images of colour and grace; she could trust this girl, she felt, who was genuine and hardworking and needy.

Outside the hall was dark. On a shelf behind a glass panel a clock kept ticking. And in the kitchen an electric light was glowing, for the kitchen was so placed that it faced the kitchen of the neighbouring flat and was thus cut off from the sun. Besides, the kitchen windows were mostly kept closed to prevent the embarrassment

and wasteful curiosity of gazing into the faces of the servants in the opposite flat. An exhaust fan, continually spinning, brought a substitute of 'fresh air' to the room. Rehman had just finished washing the dishes and pans and had laid them upside-down next to the basin, where they gleamed in the clear blue light of the fluorescent tube-light. Then he distributed heaps of rice and leftovers onto two steel plates, for himself and for the maid.

The maid was having a bath in the tiny servant's bathroom. Between splashes of water she could hear a family of pigeons cooing among the water-pipes outside. Once she heard a child crying in the neighbour's flat. She sighed to herself and rubbed her body with Pear's soap. When she opened her eyes (for she bathed with her eyes closed, as if it were a form of love-making or intimacy to which even oneself should not be witness, or as if it were a dream she had consented to dream) she gazed at the soap in her hand—a small melted substance, glimmering fragment of the real cake, which the lady had given to her out of kindness and marvelled at its infinite transparency, its inner clarity. It was truly kind of the lady to have given her Pear's and not Lifebuoy or even Sunlight. She was pampering herself thus, involved in the lather of her thoughts as her hands performed their slow cleansing, her skin streaming gradually in

the light of the electric bulb, when Rehman's voice at the door said briefly:

'Food's ready.'

Suddenly self-conscious, she pretended she was not there and did not move till she sensed he had gone. Urgently lifting the bucket and pouring the remaining water on herself, she proceeded to dry herself. Chin sunk absorbedly, she buttoned her blouse, allowing the two hollows of the blouse to scoop and lift her breasts as if they were handfuls of earth, and then quickly slipped on her petticoat. Coming into the servant's room after checking with an alert duck-like movement that Rehman was not there (she could hear him making clinking and clanking noises in the kitchen), she wound her sari loosely around herself. Finally she entered the kitchen and found Rehman had been waiting for her, but was busy posing as if he had not, occupying himself with trivial tasks like moving a saucepan slightly from left to right, or opening the door of the fridge and staring at its light and then closing it.

Without a word, they sat down on the floor in front of the two full plates and began to eat. Eating was a passionate business, beyond words. But she could not keep herself from talking.

'How hot this chilli is!' she said, having bitten into one.

Rehman laughed gruffly.

'Chillies will be hot,' he wisely replied. Then he added, 'Small chillies are the hottest.'

Once more they fell silent, intent with their fingers upon the food. Rehman was thinking, This kitchen was a quiet place before *she* came here, she's too young, will she be able to learn how to . . . how to what? Here his thoughts became vague. Anyway, the boy, Tapas, had respected him right from the start, his only fault was that he'd seen too many films and so when he'd gone away to Bombay it came as no surprise.

'Do you eat hot food in your country?' the maid asked.

Rehman's country was Bihar. His wife and children and seventy-two-year-old father lived there in a village.

'Yes,' he replied. Scornfully he remarked, 'This is nothing. The kind of food we eat makes the eyes water.' She widened her own eyes as an answer. Picking up a chilli half playfully, she asked:

'What do you call *this* in your language?'

He stared at it for a moment, seeming to measure the distance between her hand and his eyes.

'Mirrach,' he pronounced almost spitefully, and the way he spat out the word made it indeed sound dreadful.

Delighted, the maid hummed:

'Mirrach!' Then continued, 'I used to work in a

Punjabi house before. They didn't eat rice, they ate parathas.'

'Punjabis eat parathas,' mumbled Rehman, his mouth full of rice. 'One Punjabi can finish off seven or eight parathas.'

'They would give us two parathas and dal,' she said. 'But I liked to have mine with hot chutney . . . tchaa!' And she shuddered with pleasure at the thought, and made a smart smacking sound with her tongue.

Rehman looked at her as he swallowed his food. He himself had a jar of mango chutney, which the memsaab had quite forgotten about, hidden in the darkest shelf at the bottom of a cupboard. Now and then, he took it out when he was sure the memsaab was sleeping and ate some of it with a quarter of an onion and a cold leftover crescent of a chappati; when Tapas was there, he used to share it with the boy and feel fleetingly related to him. He had decided that if the memsaab should ever remember the jar, he would bring it to the table with a straight face as if nothing had happened, and if it was empty by then, he would insist with an injured smile that the memsaab had finished it long ago, or, if he was in a risky mood, pretend it had never existed. He wondered whether he should offer some of it to the maid, but concluded, not yet, he must wait and get to know her.

'O!' she exclaimed. 'I've eaten too much!'

Her plate was empty, not a grain of rice on it, no evidence but a bay leaf stained with turmeric and two split cardamom pods in a corner. So empty was the plate that it looked perfectly clean and washed, and when she leaned over it her features were reflected there unmistakably. She belched, a sound of no significance that mingled with the air. Glancing at Rehman, she smiled shyly.

'O!' she repeated. 'How much I've eaten!'

Rehman, disarmed, said:

'But have a little chutney,' in the warm, tolerant voice of a grandfather.

She looked at him in surprise.

'Do you have any?' she asked innocently.

Silently, heavily, Rehman got up. He too had finished; he rinsed his plate in the basin and quickly washed his hands. Then, with great deliberation, he turned and walked to a cupboard, seeming to follow his belly, which travelled a little way ahead of him. Sitting with some difficulty on his haunches (what a man will do when he is charmed by a woman!) he reached into the bottom shelf with a look of deep, unseeing concentration on his face, and fumbled determinedly for a few moments. At last, from a chaos of saucepans and discarded dishes, he

231

retrieved a cunningly gleaming jar whose contents—small, archaicly sliced pieces of mango—were held immobile in a golden-coloured oil.

'Here,' he said, unscrewing and unscrewing the lid, 'Achaar...'

She was overwhelmed. She carefully picked up a piece and sucked on it, her face squeezing shut at its sourness. The two said nothing to each other for a while, and she let a silent contentment spread and envelop her. Eventually, she rose to wash her plate, while Rehman sat on a stool, picking his teeth with a matchstick and spitting softly. At this point, the strange musical chimes of the doorbell rang out. 'Coming,' she sang softly and obscurely to herself. 'Coming.' She passed quickly through the servants' quarters through the connecting door to the passage. She leaned against the impressive brown-and-white front door; standing on tip-toe, she pressed an eye against the peep-hole and looked intently. But she could make out nothing; everything was dark; there was a head, yes, which looked many times larger than the body. Hesitantly, she puzzled at the lock and opened the door a little way. Outside there was a man with a jhadu in one hand and a bucket in another, a dreary blue cloth tucked around his waist and his knees.

'Who?' she asked aggressively, though her voice broke timidly at the questioning peak of the word.

'It's Panna,' called Rehman lazily from the kitchen. 'Let him in!'

She stood aside reluctantly. This man, behaving most mysteriously, ignored her and entered with a frown on his face; he stooped forward with a kind of exhaustion as he walked, which made him oddly attractive to her eyes. He went straight to the hall, took a few detours, and disappeared.

'Who is this man?' she asked as she returned to the kitchen, screwing up her eyebrows. Being new to the house, everything in it and everything that happened to it made her curious and prescient.

'Panna,' replied Rehman shortly, for he was sleepy, and could feel slumber deep in his belly. 'He cleans the bathrooms.'

Already she could not be bothered, however, for she felt sleepy herself. Where should she sleep? At random, she walked to the guest room where the ironing-board still stood from the morning with a shirt lying on its back; instinctively, she arranged the irresponsible-looking sleeves and then switched on the fan. When she turned, her eyes fell on a bad picture on the wall (the only bad picture in the house, done by a close friend of the lady's)

which showed the Bombay skyline and the Arabian Sea, in which the sky was too blue and the sea too full of waves, in which the paint had dried too quickly, it seemed, into blotches, and in which the signature, in the right-hand corner, was embarrassingly large. Yet the maid went on gazing at it for a full minute with a silent, perfect disregard for aesthetics, just enjoying the colours, all the colours travelling confidently in different directions. Then, fugitively, once, she touched it, to see what it felt like—as it was an oil painting on a canvas, it was a little rough to her finger, like an old man's cheek. After this, satisfied, she lay down on the carpet. To her right was a bed meant for a guest, and to her left a giant window in which end-of-summer clouds were swimming with a turtle-like, unapprehensive motion. Soon, she fell asleep, a small curled figure in a sari, her breath breaking now and then into snores that had a circumspect gentleness in keeping with her character.

That night, as Rehman was washing his feet in the bathroom, he noticed two flowers on the window-ledge. He allowed the water to run absent-mindedly and coldly along his ankles, and got his tucked-up trousers a little wet. Meanwhile he leaned forward to pick up the flowers. At first he was surprised and disarmed, and felt part of

a larger, ramifying mystery. Then, putting two and two together, he realized that the maid must have left them behind inadvertently that afternoon after her bath. Quite slowly, as he remembered the day, and heard, in his mind, her voice telling him about chillies, he smiled confidentially to himself. Alone in that tiny bathroom with his feet under a running tap, a modest, ruminative smile came to his lips. He could not help it.

With these two flowers, dry and dark red now, he came into the kitchen. I'll tell her tomorrow, he thought, not to leave her flowers lying about, they can't be my responsibility. A sudden curiosity seized him and he stood there still and silent for a moment in the pantry in the blue light of the fluorescent lamp, head slightly bent, sniffing at the two flowers. In his tight vest and his white working trousers (whose edges were now dark and wet), with the flowers pressed against his nose, he looked big and absurdly delicate at the same time. No, they have no smell, he concluded in an instant, and because he was used to thinking aloud, he actually said this to himself in the kitchen, though no one heard him; the lady and her husband must be asleep now. He proceeded to the dustbin in the corner and threw them into the garbage. O-ho! he thought, the garbage . . . Something like a black weariness and depression came over him, not because he

had worked too hard that day and could work no more, but because the idea of now having to drop the bag of garbage down the garbage-chute seemed to him an idea of transcendental pettiness. At the same time the lady's face, with angry eyes like Durga's, flashed before him. But something as quickly anaesthetized this fearful image and put it to sleep, leaving Rehman feeling comfortable and conscience-free. Doesn't matter, he thought, I'll do it tomorrow morning . . . The time stretching between night and next morning seemed endless and full of hope and consolation and promise. Tomorrow early morning . . . So it was that the two flowers spent the night on top of a heap of fishbones and eggshells and breadcrumbs and tea-leaves and cold rice.

# When We Moved
# to This House

When we moved to this house, my father decided to give a feast—a small feast for some relatives and close friends. My mother worked all morning in the kitchen; she did not trust the cook. She made dal and shuktani and fried savouries from potatoes and poppy seeds, a preparation from unripe jackfruit, and another of immense chunks of chittol fish, and smaller tangda fish which lay in the sauce with their eyes open. The cook tried to help, saying, all the time, 'Yes, boudi', and 'No, boudi'. Everyone who was invited came.

The first to arrive were my uncle and aunt, and then came my cousin Shanti with her husband and her little son, Bulbul, and a few moments later, Chandrima mashi and Indrani mashi, two sisters who have never

married, and who were my mother's friends at the Government High School in Sylhet, and last of all Paramesh mama, who was and still is my father's friend, with his wife, an Englishwoman from Yorkshire, whom I call Elizabeth mami.

My uncle sat on the rocking-chair and rocked, rocked, rocked himself. Bulbul, the nine-year-old boy, stood on the ski-like curved base of the rocking-chair, and rocked with my uncle. Everyone was talking—Indrani mashi about the Mahabharat and her arthritis, Chandrima mashi about her nephews, about school-children, and about the way Muslims recite their prayers on the loudspeaker, Paramesh mama about stocks and shares and the meanings of certain Sanskrit words, and my mother about herself. My aunt and my cousin were listening to my mother. From time to time, Elizabeth mami, that splendid and good-hearted lady, spoke to her neighbour, whoever it happened to be, in a strange, staccato version of Bengali, and her neighbour answered all her questions in amazement. Whenever she tried to speak the Bengali language, her Yorkshire tongue rebelled and made a crazy attempt at liberation; to say her pronunciations were *wrong* would be missing the point; they were innocent, confused, and beyond the parlance of human society, like the song of a bird.

Bulbul stopped rocking and with a serious face turned to watch Elizabeth mami speak. Outside the room, the sandals and shoes which people had taken off before they entered had grown into a glorious and variously-soled heap. So many different types of feet, such a multiplicity of sizes, such a range of taste in footwear, varying from the ascetic to the garish! Inside, the room was so populated that space itself seemed to have been crowded out.

Later, we sat round the oval glass table and ate. 'What a table, sir!' exclaimed Paramesh mama to my father. Everyone praised the food; Elizabeth mami had the richest fund of adjectives, for she had recourse to two languages. Everyone served everyone else; there was a great flurry and multiplication of hands, hands serving and passing and being used to eat with. My uncle said to me, 'I hear you cook? Is this true? Where do you get your spices in London?' I said, 'Oh, there are Bangladeshi shops, Indian shops, Pakistani shops. I'm quite a good cook, really.' Someone belched gently without drawing attention; it mingled graciously and unremarkably with the air.

Afterwards we filed in once more to the bedroom to wash our hands. Even after washing with the creamiest soap in town, a soap that itself seemed edible as cheese,

our fingers retained a smell of spices. Outside, in the hall, I saw the cook, as he took the dishes into the kitchen, expertly and almost invisibly insert a savoury into his mouth. In the hot and silent afternoon, he polished the glass table with a squelching, wet rag, standing back from time to time and winking at it with one eye closed, until, to his one open eye, it looked clean and immeasurably perfect again.

# Like a Dream

He tried to phone his friend but couldn't get the line. Sometimes there was that repetitive engaged signal—poo, poo, poo, poo, like a horn blowing in a traffic-jam. At other times there was no connection at all, only distant noises that resembled the taking-off or landing of an aircraft.

In desperation, he tried to call the operator. He couldn't get through; once or twice it rang with touching futility (a sweet, plaintive sound like singing) but no one picked it up on the other end. He kept trying. Silently he began to count to himself the number of times he tried. As he dialled, the moon might have risen above him at midday and the sun might have gone out. He wouldn't have cared. On his sixteenth attempt, he got through seemingly without a connection being made.

'Operator service,' said a woman's voice.

He asked for the number.

'Please wait,' said this voice. Then it was heard no more, it vanished from his life like childhood.

He waited. He waited and waited. He heard women, operators, laughing in the background. What are they doing, he thought. A tapping noise began, tap, tap, tap, tick, tick, tap.

'Please,' he thought.

He could not complete the sentence. It would have been a very long sentence, a very eloquent sentence. He did not bother to begin it.

'Hello,' he said. He raised his voice and repeated the word like a mantra. 'Hello! Hello! Hello?'

The women broke into otherworldly laughter. They sounded very happy. He thought of walking into the room and breaking their backs with a stick. Then they would not be so happy. But they too have mothers and fathers and sisters and brothers and perhaps husbands and even children, he thought. Sighing, he put down the phone.

He went aimlessly to the verandah and looked at some buffaloes. Then he came back and picked up the phone again. This time he found three people—one woman and two men—talking to each other in a cross-

connection, silly flies trapped in this fatal web woven by a creature called Calcutta Telephones.

'Please disconnect,' said the woman.

'I will disconnect,' said the man, 'as soon as you disconnect.'

'Will you both disconnect?' said the man.

'Who are you?' said the first man.

He listened for some time and debated with himself whether to join in or not. He longed to tell them something perfect and memorable, like the Sermon on the Mount. But he shook his head and replaced the receiver. He gazed at the phone thoughtfully. It's quite useless, he thought. A telephone in Calcutta is quite useless. He had once seen Charlie Chaplin eating a shoe with great relish in *The Gold Rush*. He had served the shoe on a plate and carved it and chewed it, picking and sucking the nails like bones. He wondered what Chaplin would have done with this telephone. Something unexpected, no doubt. Something which would have made him look at it in a new way.

'I'll see the film by myself,' he thought. 'It'll be a new experience.'

So thinking he got up and changed his shirt and went out of the house. On his way he bought a copy of

the *Statesman* from the footpath and carefully read the Cinemas-Entertainment section on the second page, the names of theatres in tiny print, Globe, Lighthouse, Minerva, Metro, Tiger. He took a mini-bus to Esplanade. As every seat was occupied, he had to stand all the way bending his head, because the bus had a low roof, which was after all why it was called a mini-bus, and he thought all the way, Any moment this man next to me will get up, but he did not.

When he got off at Esplanade, he went to the Metro cinema, the pride of all cinema-halls in the city. It was showing, surprisingly, an old black-and-white Hindi film, a classic. He was pleased, because he liked black-and-white films: in them was a world which no longer existed, a world in which a hero and heroine could burst effortlessly into a song in the middle of an empty road without a car running over them, a world in which it was possible to sing songs in a park, or in front of a house, or in a garage, or in a shop, or in front of a hospital.

He bought a ticket for a balcony seat. There was no queue because it was an old film and because ever since that terrible box, the video, had entered people's living rooms, cinema-halls had fallen empty. He walked up the stairs.

The place seemed more or less deserted. The bar which sold cold drinks and popcorn looked old. He went in through a door. It was dark, and a documentary was being shown, about the construction of a new dam. An old usher peered at his ticket with a torch and guided him to a seat. He sat down. He looked at the screen. Water was rushing, swirling, flowing everywhere. It looked white and frothy, like milk. Labourers were walking around with spades and iron baskets full of stones on their head. Then there were engineers in big machines, shouting orders and pointing, it seemed, to the sun. There was something religious about them. An intolerable tune that was neither foreign nor Indian but was a terrible demented hybrid that could not stop drawing attention to itself played on and on, with drums and guitars and banjos and flutes. In the end, climactically, the dam rose. The voice of the commentator called it 'a noble achievement'. Things were said about 'the new India' and 'our scientists and engineers, of whom we are proud'. He sat there looking at the dam but could not feel anything, pride or anger.

He began to feel hot. The air-conditioners weren't running, and standing, revolving fans were noisily blowing towards him and then temperamentally away from him. The hall looked old and stately, like a palace,

with parts of its walls carved to resemble icing on a cake.

After a few minutes, he heard muffled sounds of protest at the back, and he saw a couple walk past him swiftly and then out of the door. He could hear an argument outside. At last the film began, and he settled into his seat. The credits came on.

He was completely relaxed now, in spite of the heat. He began to hum with the first song. It was all about a woman's eyes, and was very witty. He felt himself being drawn into that black-and-white world, in which the cars were all Plymouths and Bentleys, and the heroine was a pampered only child who played badminton, and the hero was a coarse but gentle taxi-driver with a mind of his own. He thought that the world in those days must have really been simple and black and white, that no colour existed in those days, and that people were made then from light and shadow, and so was the world.

By chance he saw something dark and small and furtive pass along the first row. He wondered what it could be. He turned his eyes again to the film. Then he saw it, nearer this time. It was a rat, a small bundle of brown hair and eyes and life. It disappeared beneath a seat. Casually, quite calmly, he raised his legs and put them on the seat in front of him, in which fortunately no

one was sitting. The heroine was very beautiful in spite of the fact that she played badminton, but he couldn't forget the rat.

Then he saw another and another, like dark sparks travelling from one end of the hall to the other. Many of them were about. He wondered if they were looking for something, and whatever it was, it must be extremely important. Suddenly he rose from the seat and walked down the aisle towards the door. He did not feel anyone looking at him because there was hardly anyone in the hall, except for those very busy creatures whom, out of an inexplicable sense of respect, he did not wish to disturb. Outside it was hot and sunny. His eyes took time to get used to the light, as if he had just woken up. Today has been like a dream, he thought, but glancing at his watch he saw it was three-thirty in the afternoon, and immediately he wondered what he would do next.

# Coolness

The power-cut had begun at seven in the morning. Now it was twelve. It was Saturday.

The man was standing in his underwear by the window. Two hours ago he had taken off his trousers, and half an hour later, his shirt. Still he was sweating profusely.

Thank God I'm a man, he thought, would it be possible to do this if I was a woman?

After some time, he took off his vest quite unconsciously, and then his underpants; it was a while before he noticed he was naked. He wandered around his room thus, enjoying himself. He hummed to himself tunelessly a song by Tagore:

A bee drifts into my room, murmuring.
It tells me of someone—then, disappears.

He stopped to contemplate himself in the mirror. He felt a faraway, paternal compassion for his body, with its awkwardly sloping shoulders, its two nipples like gentle eyes gazing at him, the embarrassing feminine way in which the waist curved slightly into the hips.

> Beneath the light of some unknown sky
> Madhavi flowers blossom in a secret forest . . .
> The messenger-bee comes to me, bringing news
> Of that blossoming, humming it in my ears.

He spattered talcum powder on himself till his neck and shoulders and chest and nipples and belly were white, and only the navel remained black and bottomless. His hand made an affectionate slapping noise as he tried to powder the inaccessible portions of his back. It was obvious the man loved himself and the feel of himself in his modest way. His voice shook a little as he sang. Mysterious clouds of talcum powder rose and vanished around his shoulders. All this the mirror captured in its frame in a series of transient cloud-like instants. The room smelt of lavender.

Now the man entered the bath. He turned on the cold-water tap and found the water amazingly hot. He checked to see if it was the hot water tap he had turned

on; but no. Undaunted, he filled to the brim a pink plastic mug and doused himself experimentally. He blubbered in anguish. In between his blubbering he still sang tunelessly, a little loudly now so that he could hear himself above the water.

> How should I remain content in this room? My
>     mind
> Is quicksilver, troubled. I've lost count
> Of how these days pass—days spent in counting
>     days.

A few minutes later, he came out of the bath without drying himself. Silver drops of water ran down his walnut-coloured skin. He stood in front of the window in an easterly breeze, and his arms and elbows and knees and testicles seemed to weep.

> A deep enchantment falls on me. I lose
> All interest in my work. My hours are caught
> In a web of songs, a skein of music. The bee
> Tells me of someone, then—disappears.

He allowed his body to cool. Cool as a shade in a forest, cool as a flower in the shade of a forest. In the breeze,

naked and gleaming, he shivered as if a woman had kissed him.

'Aaah,' he sang, with a hint of melody. 'Aaah.'

He was sure no one could see him.